a tasty selection

from the

Yorkshire Writers' Lunch:

Andrew Shephard

Annabel Howarth

Clair Wright

Dave Rigby

Emma Harding

Inez Cook

Suzanne Hudson

Virginia Hainsworth

Published by Hilltop Communications

ISBN: 978-0-9932669-2-8

MENU

A CHEEKY COCKTAIL

the perfect start to the perfect read

APPETISERS

moreish morsels to tickle your taste buds

STARTERS AND LIGHT BITES

entertaining reads that won't spoil your appetite

SEAFOOD PLATTER

taste the sea with these fishy tales

MAIN COURSES

hearty reads to get your teeth into and some serious food for thought

SIDE DISHES

ideal reading accompaniments

DESSERTS

make room for these lip-smacking puddings

DIGESTIF

loosen those reading buttons with this aid to digestion

PETIT FOURS

indulge a sweet tooth with these dainty treats

AFTERNOON TEA

time to put your feet up with a nice cup of tea and a piece of cake

WHY THE YORKSHIRE WRITERS' LUNCH?

Emma Harding

We're a (small) community of writers both published and aspiring, based in Yorkshire. We meet weekly for lunch and a discussion of what motivates us to write, what prevents us from writing, what we've learnt and what we've written. In between mouthfuls of sandwich, burger or wrap, with the odd jacket potato thrown in.

We decided to create a shared blog for many reasons. To help some of us take our first tentative steps into the blogosphere. To give us the chance to see what effect exposure to the bright glare of (potential) readers has on our writing. To create a regular commitment – something which some of us really need to give us the impetus to put words on a page.

And because we have found that it helps to help each other.

Writing is, of course, a solitary activity. How could it be anything else? It's just you, your pen and paper. Or keyboard and screen. Or quill and parchment if that's what floats your boat.

When it's going well the solitude is part of the joy – the quiet exploration of your own head to discover the worlds you might create, the characters you could breathe into life, the emotions you want to evoke in your readers. Even if the only reader is you. But when it's an off day, it can feel like you're screaming into an empty room and hearing the echoes of your creative failures bouncing back at you from every surface.

In this state, mutual encouragement and support are required, are even mandatory. It is how we turn our struggles and our doubts into better writing, perhaps even competition winning or publishable writing. It's how we garner the courage to pick up our chosen writing implement once more and try again.

This is why we lunch. And why we blog together too.

You can find us at yorkshirewriterslunch.blogspot.co.uk

WHY DINING ON WORDS?

After a year and a half of weekly lunching and blogging, we've decided to publish the fruits of our labours in printed form.

Because there's something so much more satisfying about an actual book, rather than a webpage, isn't there?

So here is *Dining on WORDS*, a veritable smorgasbord of poetry, short stories, flash fiction, travel tales and comment. There are even three collaborative pieces, where we each contributed a portion of the story to the overall dish. Something of an experiment, certainly, but hopefully not a case of too many cooks!

Whether you're a hungry bookworm, ravenous for a good read, an aspiring writer looking for some tasty titbits or someone who just likes to kick back once in a while with a toothsome treat, there's plenty here for you to feast on.

Bon appétit.

A CHEEKY COCKTAIL

the perfect start to the perfect read

WHY READ?

Virginia Hainsworth

"I have never read a whole book in all my life."

I recently overheard someone confessing to that. We are all different (thank goodness), but what a loss it would be never to have read even one book from cover to cover.

To read is to lose oneself in another world. To sink between the covers, to envelope oneself in layer upon layer of finely crafted phrases. Like wild swimming, you launch yourself into unknown waters and swim, letting the words wash over you. Letting the language nibble at your toes, immersing yourself in someone else's imagination. With some books, it is enough to float along the surface for ages, buoyed up by the temperature of the writing. It may be cool enough to prick at your skin or it may be warmed by the sun to soothe and smooth. With some books, however, you need to dive beneath the surface head first, then kicking deeper, feel the weight of the developing story. You need to explore the characters' depths, coming up for air now and then to contemplate the emerging storyline and see how far you have travelled.

To read is to leave your current environment behind completely, if only for a while. Your book is your magic carpet. It can spirit you away to foreign lands, introducing you to new characters. You can experience the exotic, the dangerous, the seductive, without leaving your comfort zone. You can wrap yourself in the improbable, even the impossible. You can have your intellect, your beliefs and your imagination challenged.

The first words can ease you into the beginning of the story or they can catapult you right into the middle of the narrative. Your author can take you by the hand and accompany you on the journey or they can push you into the darkness and seemingly abandon you in the midst of words strung together to excite and charm you.

Your feet can be on the floor of a packed London Underground carriage, whilst your head is roaming the Namib desert. Maybe your body is curled up safely on your sofa, whilst your mind has been released into the deserted alleyways of Victorian London at midnight, your ears straining to hear the sound of pursuing footsteps. If you are trapped in a prison cell, a book can transport you through the grey walls and deposit you on the shores of a lake in Northern Canada, where you can feel free. Maybe you are confined to a hospital bed. Allow yourself to be ensconced in words which have the power to heal your soul and restore your body.

I was witness to another conversation, wherein a father was bemoaning the type of books his young son was reading. They were not, in his view, of good enough quality.

"Well," observed the boy's mother. "At least, he's reading."

I couldn't agree more.

APPETISERS

moreish morsels to tickle your taste buds

HATCHING

Clair Wright

I am empty-handed, and so
I go for a walk,
Amongst the sticky buds and poking green
I find it -
Smooth as stone
An enigma sealed tight
Taut with possibility.
Don't grasp,
It will crush
Leaving nothing.
I nurture it, warm it,
Hold it close as a secret
Mindful as a new mother
I turn it over, examine it for signs
Of what it will become.
I watch.

And it begins.
Don't hurry it
Don't force it into the light
It will burn in the glare of exposure.
It emerges
Reveals its nascent form
I touch it, hear its breath,

Feel its heartbeat.
It stumbles,
An imperfect, uncertain thing
Unfurling, pulsing with the life I gave it.
It flutters,
Stutters across the page
And takes flight.

THE BUS TO BOTHWAYS

Andrew Shephard

Country pub, left in a daze
(Well, it was my holidays)
I see a bus stop in the distance
And ask a local for assistance.
"How long until the bus to Bothways?
I don't mind if I go the longways,
But please don't point me wrongways.
And does the bus return on Sundays?"

The farmer looked me up and down
As if I were a circus clown.
"I wouldn't journey there on Sundays,
(Unless you want to come back Mondays)
You're facing backwards, anyways
The bus goes southerly to Bothways.
And more, you can't go dressed like that
In fancy spats and silk cravat.
And if you see a Bothways cat
Be sure to doff your trilby hat."

I scratched my chin in some confusion
(It may have been the beer infusion)
Looked up and down the leafy lane
And climbed aboard when green bus came.
I fell into a summer slumber
Until... a hand upon my shoulder.

"Tickets please! What destination?"
I felt for change with hesitation.
"Return to… Bothways, if you be kind.
That damned place so hard to find
Has placed a cloud upon my mind
And made my brow with furrow lined."

The clippie looked me up and down
As if I were a circus clown.
"I'm sorry, no return on Sundays
(Unless you want to come back Mondays)
You're heading wrongways, anyways.
Southerly runs the route to Bothways.
But when you go, don't dress like that
In silver spats and cream cravat.
And for God's sake, if you see a cat,
Please don't forget to doff your hat."

THE HOTHOUSE

Emma Harding

Mr and Mrs Roper, do please sit down. I'm Mr Hardy, Mike, Joachim's English teacher. It's lovely to finally meet you. Would you like some tea?

Now then, as I said on the phone, Joachim is delightful to teach, quiet, very polite and attentive in class. But there are aspects of his behaviour that we do need to discuss. No, no, Mr Roper he's doing just fine academically, he's passed all the key stage tests quite satisfactorily. Yes, it's wonderful that you're so supportive, having parents willing you to succeed is such a bonus. My concern is more about his engagement in the non-academic areas of school life. He doesn't appear to want to join in with the other pupils, he keeps himself very much to himself, preferring to stay indoors and study rather than going outside at break-time.

Of course, Mrs Roper, that's very true, to get anywhere in life you do need to study hard and not get distracted from your ambition. That's why I'm here after all. But it is surely important to have interests outside school work, isn't it? Piano? Really? Well that's wonderful. And Mandarin too? Goodness. Yes it would appear he has plenty to occupy him outside school. However that's not really what I'm saying. Well, what I'm trying to say and yes, you're quite right Mr Roper, I do need to make my point more clearly and succinctly. Yes, of course, we are all busy people aren't we? I am concerned that Joachim is not getting the chance to have fun, to enjoy life before the responsibilities that come with being an adult fall upon his shoulders.

I appreciate, Mrs Roper, that getting him into Oxford or Cambridge is your first priority and that you don't want him to be distracted from that laudable aim. But surely, and you must understand I mean no disrespect and I do realise of course that it is for you to determine the future of your son and not me and that the fees you pay for him to get the best education are considerable, but surely there will be plenty of time for books and study and libraries and crammer lessons when he's older. Surely now is the time for him to be able to play.

He is, after all, Mr and Mrs Roper, only seven.

PICS, POPHS AND ZOMBIES

Andrew Shephard

Yesterday I was walking down a track by a field. About fifty rooks had gathered in some trees beside the track and were making a hell of a racket in the low afternoon sunshine. It was like they were all talking at once about some massive breaking news in rook-world. Rooks are social creatures, and so are we.

The daily walks with Jerry, my Golden Retriever, are an essential part of my writing process. When I set off from the house I don't think about anything in a conscious way. Then, usually about half way through the walk, or when fifty rooks strike up a conversation, some ideas ping into my head like notifications on a mobile phone. It may be a scene in a chapter which needs changing, an idea for a blog post, or a few lines of a poem. For me, sitting down at a computer or a pad of paper does not usually produce inspiration. I need the free thinking time first.

After the country track, my walk takes me by some houses and across a busy road. Occasionally I meet a human being, but the urban world is mostly filled with pics, pophs, and zombies. Pics are 'people in cars'. They are busy and distracted. I was one of them once. Pophs are 'people on phones'. Sometimes the pics and pophs are one and the same. Zombies have a fixed stare and don't often make eye contact. You can spot them by thin plastic wires coming out of their ears. Crossing the road, I half tripped over some bits of plastic, the remains of broken car trim.

When I got home, I wrote this haiku down before I took my shoes off.

Cigarette, sun, mobile phone
Car crash line goes dead.
Rearrange everything.

NIGHT LIGHT

Virginia Hainsworth

It is night time in Krokom, a village in northern Sweden. Minus 22 degrees. I am standing outside and looking up into the sky.

What I can see takes my breath away.

The night sky has decided, on this rare evening, to dance.

Green swathes of what seems like fairy dust are sweeping backwards and forwards, and from left to right, becoming lighter in colour and then darker again. Shards of pale green hang from the highest point in the sky down to the horizon, swaying like delicate silk curtains, moved by an unseen and unfelt breeze. It is utterly mesmerising.

The sky is bathed in green crystals. I gaze up at the strands of phosphorescent light waltzing across their stage. Shafts of light the colour of moss break free and chase each other across the darker green mantle, only to turn around and repeat their silent manoeuvres.

Huge bands of forest green move sedately, gliding diagonally across the firmament and then quicken, as if suddenly hurrying, turning to emerald on their journey.

The heavens are on fire but burning green instead of red, as the beautifully choreographed spectacle continues. Time stands still. Only the silent sky is moving.

I never knew there were so many shades of green. Emerald. Jade. Sea-green. And more. As one band of fairy dust swoops down towards the horizon, another emerges from the left to take centre stage. But only for an instant, as it too blows away across the sky, to be replaced by a stronger band of a different hue, then dying into the distance.

As one shaft of light swirls this way and that, another spins around and shimmers towards it, as if taunting it. Like a swarm of tiny pine-green birds, each one individually unseen, but magnificent when flying together across the sky.

Each move is more stunning than the last. No still or moving picture, no computer generated image, no brilliantly painted canvas or carefully designed fabric could ever match the glory of what I am witnessing. I feel so small and insignificant under this exquisitely moving canopy. And yet, at the same time, I feel hugely privileged, to think that what is an elusive phenomenon has chosen this one night on which to emerge from its shy retreat and perform.

How good it is to be alive.

KINGS OF THE WORLD
Suzanne Hudson

Eleven pairs of boots dangling down,
A well-deserved lunch break and rest,
Far above the city's rooftops,
We sit and survey our handiwork.

A drink and a joke and a smoke,
Companionable chat and mutual respect,
The honest dignity of a hard day's work,
And a view not many have seen.

Up here we feel like the kings of the world,
Building the future but alive in the present,
Our skyscraper will join many others,
But for us it will always stand proud.

We were born to move and create with our hands,
And we do so six days a week,
Our limbs may ache with exhaustion,
But our faces reveal a proud satisfaction.

Eleven pairs of boots dangling down,
Long since lost, rotted and vanished,
But our fingers will linger on those bricks forever,
And our spirits still soar above the New York skyline.

Inspired by the famous black and white photo:
Lunch atop a Skyscraper (1932).

BLOGLESS

Clair Wright

There are days, like today, when there is nothing there at all.

This is what it would have been like for Lucy, if, pushing through the moth-ball scented fur coats, she found only the wooden back of the wardrobe.

This is how it would have been for Cinderella, if the pumpkin stayed vegetable and the mice stayed rodent.

This is how it would have been if Alice had not fallen down the rabbit hole, or if Harry had stayed in the cupboard under the stairs.

If Aladdin rubbed the lamp, and it just got shinier, he would have felt like this. Domestically satisfied, possibly, at a job done efficiently. But imaginatively, an empty vessel.

Washing done, ironing done, spellings tested, reading books laboured over. Words – unwritten. Not just unwritten – unthought, undreamt, unscribbled on a receipt in the bottom of my bag, un-tapped into my smartphone.

There are plenty of words, washing around my head like socks in the suds, but they are the wrong kind of words. They are lists, and more lists, must-dos and mustn't forgets, reproaches and regrets. These bullies push out the others - the shyer, more tentative words. They squash them, leave them crushed flat, wrung out by the unstoppable slosh and spin of Monday, Tuesday, Wednesday… you get the idea.

Those delicate, fragile words, spun from the gossamer-light, extravagant stuff of wonder, play, ponder, and idleness cannot survive such rough treatment. They are holiday words, Sunday words, free-time, free-head words. There is no room for them here.

So I am forced to write about writing nothing, just so I am writing something.

I feel better already.

STARTERS AND LIGHT BITES

entertaining reads that won't spoil your appetite

IT'S ONLY A STORY...?

Inez Cook

My three year old son loves stories. I don't just mean the weekly library trip and bedtime storybooks - he has a real love of spoken stories. He asks me or my husband to tell them several times a day, often the same ones repeated. It's also a measure of closeness. You know you're in his most trusted circle when he asks you to tell him a story (Nan and Auntie Ria have recently been invited to join these inner echelons).

When I start to think about the stories themselves, I realise they aren't just something enjoyable and entertaining. He really needs these stories. One of his favourites at the moment goes something like this:

"Mum, you know that story about when Nan was a little girl and she was on her red bike and then she fell off and got an ouch on her knee and then her mummy put some cream on her knee and gave her a plaster? Can you do that story please?"

He usually asks for it immediately after he's hurt himself. It functions to help him process the experience, as well as to understand that other people have painful experiences too, that they deal with them and then move on. He also gets to relish the idea that his silver-haired nan was once a fearless pigtailed girl zooming down a hill.

As well as working through real experiences, stories help him to work through and diffuse imaginary fears. The other evening he was quite alarmed by the tigers that were in the room. When I asked for their specific location he whispered intently that they were in the top of his body. So we made a story where we took turns to pull a tiger out of his mouth, count to three and blow each one out of the window.

Since moving house in July we've had lots of maintenance people coming to fix things and we've also had two car breakdowns. So a major theme over the summer was mending and problem-solving. This bred a whole miscellany of stories about boilers, screwdrivers, magic garden walls and breakdown trucks. I also took it as a sneaky opportunity to subtly challenge gender stereotypes in job roles, as so many maintenance workers he had encountered were men. So in our story repertoire we now have female characters such as Sarah the crane driver, who crops up whenever a vehicle gets stuck in mud, and Sue the car-loader driver who gets a fair bit of air-time during motorway journeys.

This Christmas my son will become a big brother for the first time. In the lead up to him having a sibling, we've done lots of stories and photos about when he/Mum/Dad/Nan/Granddad was a baby. Songs have proved to be good for 'new baby' story inspiration too. Stevie Wonder's *Isn't She Lovely* appears on one of our car compilation CDs and so we told him the story of the song's inception. Our embellished version has Stevie going to the hospital to meet his new baby daughter, giving her a name, counting her tiny fingers and toes and then going home to write a song for her on his piano.

Stories also provide a living connection to family memories and heritage. My husband is from Kosovo, and he often tells our son tales about his childhood growing up in a mountain village with a smallholding. He has endless material on the idylls and hardships of this kind of rural life, bordering into fairy-tale territory: falling out of cherry trees into bramble bushes, spotting an elusive wolf or bear on the mountainside, caring for and learning to ride horses or chopping logs in time for the bitterly cold winters.

When I'm asked for the seventh time that day to do the 'road builders' story and I sigh inside (it's my own fault for making that one so boring), I forget how much all this storytelling has taught me about creativity. It's helped me to reconcile that caring for my son full-time and wanting to write are not necessarily two endeavours in opposition to each other. Creative writing isn't only something I do sitting at a desk in solitude, undisturbed and under ideal solemn conditions. It's more messy than that.

Then there's the joy of improvising and the unexpected. Can I slip in a funny new detail and will he notice? How can I interrupt the usual words of the story and make it silly and fresh? How many orange-y things can I replace a traffic cone with? "Was it a fox? A squirrel? A tangerine? A tiger?" (cue giggles from my son). Or there's the collaborative aspect, where my son slots in all kinds of weird and wonderful alternate endings. In actual fact, he's the one teaching me about stories and the art of storytelling.

Spinning these yarns has really underlined for me how intimate, even sacred, the act of storytelling is. What could be more intimate than sharing an imaginary space with another person, with all that that entails emotionally along a narrative journey? There's a sense, especially with oral storytelling, that we're making something unique and unrepeatable. Being entertained is almost secondary to sharing together something fundamental to being human and making sense of the world.

PARADISE LOST

Andrew Shephard

Down at the bottom of the Northern Line
Is a thirties estate where the weather is fine.
Dad gets the tube at seven-thirty
And Mum stays at home so that nothing gets dirty.

Mock Tudor houses have lawns and wooden fences
Streets are lined with blossom trees, parks have bins and benches.
Gutter sparrows cheep all day, ash cans clash and crunch
A rag and bone man's carthorse has a nose bag for his lunch.

Out of school, friends roam the park: would we see the flasher?
We splodge along the River Wandle looking for some treasure.
I know I live in Paradise, I've been up North you see:
Granddad's house is black with soot, you go outside to pee.

My sister, tall and grown up, she says we live in Mordor
And eating greens at Sunday lunch is a form of torture.
There's a scene, I go upstairs, the box room of the house
And listen to the radio with Georgy Girl, my mouse.

My sister has a boyfriend, disapproved by Mother
They only go out to the stock cars if she takes her brother.
I have to go to keep the peace, I sit all quiet and squirm
But secretly it is good fun to watch them crash and burn.

She says: I want to die, I hate this place, she calls me "ugly toad".
I say: I'll marry Zena Marsh and live just down the road.
My sister lived in Mordor, but me I lived in Heaven:
Sister dear was sweet sixteen and I was just eleven.

***

I read in the paper about a North-South divide in house prices. The divide is not new, but over time it takes different forms. I grew up in a North-South divide household in a London suburb. My father was a displaced, domino-playing Yorkshireman. My mother was a committed southerner, and hated it when we travelled too far north. She associated the North with grime and poverty. I loved the trips to Bradford when I visited my grandparents because it was a completely different world, one where I struggled to understand what people were saying; a world which provided a sharp contrast, visually, with my modern suburban surroundings.

THE WALK

Dave Rigby

I stand under the petrol station canopy, watching the rain as it bounces off the already deep puddles and wonder if the walk was such a good idea after all.

Planning it in the dry and warmth of the kitchen, maps laid out across the table it had seemed straightforward. Catch the train, get off, walk, find somewhere to stay – a short break without any real planning.

But I'd forgotten to allow for the rain – and I call myself a walker.

I finish the last mouthful of BLT sandwich, my gourmet lunch courtesy of the garage shop. I take off my rucksack and reach in for my waterproof trousers. Balancing on one booted foot, the other comes to a halt half-way through its journey down the trouser leg. I almost topple, but manage to force my foot through to freedom. The second foot is no easier. I'm sweating and tell myself for the umpteenth time to take my boots off before going through this performance.

Mission completed, I rest against some bags of barbecue charcoal and get my breath. Gloves on, hat on, complete with ear flaps. I set off again, through the forecourt mini-lake, to reach the safety of the pavement and walk west. I hear a bus struggling up the hill behind me and instinctively stick out a hand. I'm in luck, there's a stop close by and the bus waits for me.

As we make slow progress through the mist and murk,

I begin to overheat and only then remember to take off my hat, gloves and jacket. The trousers are staying on, however warm it gets. Gradually the rain eases and then, miraculously, stops. I press the bell and step off the bus into the dry. I pinpoint the village on my still soggy map, cross the road, find the waymarker and I'm off. The sun gradually eases through the clouds as I pass the gas plant and head for the sea. The lighthouse stands alone, retired and a little the worse for wear. It's now hot and in tee-shirt and waterproof trousers, I walk miles along the deserted beach, amused by the frequent signs which tell me the sand dunes are unstable cliffs to be avoided. There's a sound of oystercatchers, and far out across the bay, the sight of the slowly turning blades of the windfarm.

Hours later I'm peering through the fading evening light at the 'Vacancies' sign of a B&B. The downpour has restarted and I stand in rain-slicked clothes and ear-flapped hat, water dripping from my bearded chin, waiting for someone to answer the door. Eventually it opens and a large man wearing a buttoned waistcoat beneath a green cardigan eyes me apprehensively. Whatever guest test he's setting, I don't pass muster. He tells me that unfortunately, he only has a family suite available, that I'll have to try elsewhere. But when a casual question, as I'm departing, elicits the crucial information that I'm walking the Welsh Coastal Path, a single room suddenly materialises. He tells me it's quite a challenge, all 870 miles of it. I nod and agree.

The Taj Mahal is brightly lit and as I rehydrate with Indian lager and put another forkful of potato and spinach curry in my mouth, I study the map and plan the second - and final - day of my epic walk.

THE ART AND CRAFT OF WRITING

Emma Harding

Is writing an art or a craft? Does it come from natural talent or hard graft? Are you born a writer or can you learn to become one?

Recent debate about the value of creative writing courses – stirred up by Hanif Kureshi who disputed whether such courses could ever deliver good writing (despite teaching one himself) – has pondered the perennial question of whether writing is something that can be taught. Or is it the case that you've either got it or you haven't?

But this debate's based on a false premise. That writing is a single process – have an idea ... write it down. When actually it's (at least) two. Writing and editing. Two separate activities. Demanding different skills. And when you look at it that way, it's clear that writing is both an art and a craft.

You need to have a story to tell, an interesting perspective on the world, a head full of engaging characters. No one else can put those ideas in your head. Of course this is not to say that ideas are formed in a vacuum. All ideas are sparked by external stimuli – the people you meet, the experiences you have, the things you see. But how these stimuli percolate through you and coalesce into an idea for a story is all down to you and no one else.

But then you have to get that idea onto the page. You

have to write it down.

I saw Michael Morpurgo on TV recently talking about this aspect of writing:

"The best thing to do is to talk a story – from your head … down your arm through your fingers onto the page and you let it flow which means mistakes and all. You don't worry about the spelling, the punctuation. I'm sorry but you don't. Not the first time. You just get the stupid thing down there. I think it's rather like an artist sketching. When an artist is sketching it's letting the line flow, capturing somehow the image of it. And that's what I do - I tell it onto the page and craft it afterwards."

I think many new writers, including me, focus on the first part of this process - the capturing of the story. There is a tendency, perhaps, to think that once it's down on the page the job is done. But, as Morpurgo says, this is just a sketch, an outline of the true story that's waiting to be revealed.

And just as an artist uses a palette of colours and materials to build on that sketch, give it form and shape, light and dark, texture and depth, so the writer has a palette of words. An almost infinite palette.

It's at this point then when the work (and fun?) really begins. The work of editing, of crafting the text into shape. There's real skill to this, it takes patience and practise. It's about choosing the right word for the job, word by word, sentence by sentence, page by page.

In her (thoroughly recommended) book, *Reading like a Writer,* Francine Prose demonstrates how it is this deliberate and often painstaking word selection process that is the real skill:

"For any writer, the ability to look at a sentence and see

what's superfluous, what can be altered, revised, expanded and, especially, cut, is essential."

She uses extracts from a range of literary examples to illustrate (and encourage) the calculated crafting that makes great writing great. And which makes writing a joy.

Perhaps the key role of the creative writing course then - alongside the vital element of encouragement and support - is to help develop the skill of editing rather more than the talent of writing. To help inexperienced writers turn their very individual ideas and stories into finished, polished works, ready for a more public readership.

What do you think? Are you an artist or a craftsperson? Do you think someone can learn to be a writer?

LE TOUR DE HUDDERSFIELD

Andrew Shephard

The town lies below me in the valley, a star-shape of grey slate and stone framed by the green hills. I'm anonymous in the *peloton*, hidden away by my team. The break-away at the front is just for show, and the task of the moment is a safe, high-speed descent to the ring road and into town. The wind, loud in my ears, almost drowns out the noise of the crowd.

I glimpse flags and faces through the pack of riders. Hunched over the bars and hiding in the slipstream of the bikes ahead of me, I rest my legs for the climb that I know will come all too soon. It's a climbing day. It's not the Pyrenees, no, but the laws of physics and human biology dictate that I will spend much more time going up than going down.

All too soon, I'm on my way back out of the town. The climb starts gently enough, a smooth incline waking up the muscles for the torture that lies ahead. The gap between one bike and another grows, centimetre by centimetre as the strain begins to tell. The nonchalant smiles of the easy descent have been replaced with grim expressions of concentration. A nod from a cyclist in the same shirt as mine gives me the signal. He starts to pull me through the pack. It's time to attack. I increase my effort, refusing to look at the hill rearing up like a dragon ahead of me.

In a matter of minutes I am at the head of the *peloton* with my team-mate and we set off after the doomed break-away, a ragged quartet already in our field of vision. I enter a tunnel, a tunnel of focus and faces, head down, rhythmic, welcoming the pain in my legs and the screams of my muscles. I'm not faster or fitter, but I can take the pain better than some. The break-away riders fall away dispirited in my wake, mere chip papers fluttering in the gutter.

The noise of the blood rushing through my veins reaches a crescendo like the end of a symphony, but there is a final flourish of the timpani as the hill turns a corner and gets steeper still. My calf muscles threaten a strike, but I see a red banner which means the end is close, and laugh my way home along the last undulating kilometre. My teammate waves me on, with a 'job done' look of satisfaction on his face.

When I cross the finish line I almost fall off my bike at the sudden loss of forward momentum. I'm instantly surrounded by a crowd of reporters and TV cameras, my precious air breathed by people who need it less than me.

Somehow I find the strength to open the garage and put my bike away.

"How was your ride?" says my wife. "Who came to lunch today?"

"Please," I say, legs trembling. "I need a moment. Everywhere you go in Huddersfield it's nothing but bloody hills."

WRITE TIME

Suzanne Hudson

"So have you got any New Year's resolutions?" people ask each other at this time of year and I recently found myself offering up the same one as last year and the year before that.

"To write more," I said and even though I meant it sincerely, I cringed inwardly as I said it. Because I have been here before, too many times and I knew deep down that my hopes were doomed.

Or are they? I don't know if it is the eternal optimist in me, but something has felt a bit different in the last few days. As a teacher, I have enjoyed the last two weeks off work, and the leisurely lie-ins and general laziness of my Christmas holidays have resulted in a strange phenomenon.

During the evening, I find my mind firing up, ready to create. By the time I get into bed I am positively buzzing with ideas. As I turn out the light I have to fight the urge to get up and turn on my laptop. I feel like I could write all night.

Perplexed by this strange turn of events, I reached out to the community of the internet. Surely I couldn't be the only one with these nocturnal yearnings?

A few clicks later, I found the confirmation that I needed. A guest blog post by Jonathan Manor on Jeff Goins' blog about writing (goinswriter.com/night-writing) revealed that there are plenty of writers, bloggers and freelancers, for whom the twilight hours are a hotbed of creativity.

Manor questions the received wisdom that the morning is the best time to write and explains that, for him, writing at night works best, *"...because it's devoid of distraction, there's nothing else left to do in the day, there's no one else to hurry to. It's simply just you being yourself and pouring out the emotions that you've gathered from your daytime experience and using that creativity to create something beautiful and interesting."*

Further reading on the topic led me to Matt Shoard's blog post on *Writing at Night,* which reveals a long list of famous authors who wrote at night, including Tennessee Williams, Charles Dickens and TS Eliot (theguardian.com /books/booksblog/2010/dec/21/writing-at-night).

I had thought that my lack of productivity during the day was due to a lethal mix of perfectionism, procrastination and a general lack of willpower. But looking back I see that the reason most of my first drafts are written in the evening is simply because I am responding to my natural writing rhythms. While redrafting and editing are fine for me as daytime activities, my initial creative burst needs to happen at nightfall.

All day long I have been trying to write this blog post. I had no idea what to write and I felt that I had nothing to say. At 8.30pm it suddenly came to me and flowed out with ease. So my New Year's resolution has been retained but extended slightly. 'Write more, but at the right time.' And the next time I have an urge to create as I turn out the light, I will get up and write.

A GERMAN CHRISTMAS MARKET
or a tale of two cities
Virginia Hainsworth

Imagine this: a haze of red, blue and green fairy lights blurred by the rising steam from spicy, heady glühwein. The muted sound of a tasteful Christmas carol, sung in its native German. Woollen-clad shoppers huddled together like penguins. The warm sweet smell of hot doughnuts beckoning passers-by, calling us over to sample them.

Imagine these things. And yes I was trying to imagine them as I sat in the back of a stationary taxi cab, en route from Hamburg Airport to Lübeck. The mist I saw was not that arising from glühwein, but that of the car windows steaming up as the snowstorm began. The lights were not fairylike at all. They were the tail lights of other cars, winking at me through the falling snowflakes of a surprise blizzard. Not quite what I had envisioned.

The Lübeck of my imagination was a far cry from the reality of this white-hot traffic jam. I was trapped on sheet ice, watching the silent dance of lorries jack-knifing and cars shimmying towards each other, bumpers kissing bumpers in unplanned and un-choreographed routines.

I eventually arrived safely in Lübeck and was welcomed in via the Holstentor, a twin towered medieval gate. The gate was illuminated by the moonlight and appeared one moment as a magical form of transportation back over hundreds of years, yet fleetingly resembling a huge bouncy castle, minus its children, standing forlorn against the night sky. A strange, memorable contrast.

As I wandered through the narrow streets, the Lübeck Christmas Market revealed itself exactly as I had imagined it. Row upon row of stalls selling tree decorations, advent stars, tree lights, candle holders; all gleaming like festive jewels of emerald, ruby and gold. All designed to enhance the perfect Christmas interior. All designed to create their own special memories for the future, with promises to adorn our homes for years of Christmases to come.

And then another stark contrast. Surely that could not be the harsh sound of a tinny rendition of 'Jingle Bells' emerging from someone's hat! The traditional sounds of the market seemed to recede as I looked at the cheap red felt hat, complete with reindeer antlers and bells. The wearer stood motionless as the hat sang its little Christmas heart out. As the climax of the song approached, so as not to be ignored, the antlers started to flap in time to the music, quivering as the manufactured singing voice attempted a shaky vibrato.

It was impossible not to laugh – at the hat, as it began its unrequested encore and at myself as I queued up to buy one!

Lübeck was enchanting me yet again. A tale of two cities, bringing the imagination to life, with a couple of Christmas surprises thrown in.

PERFECTLY IMPERFECT

Annabel Howarth

"I am perfectly imperfect."

That is my new mantra. It has taken me 41 years to reach this point of being. It is so enlightening and uplifting and is helping me feel happier and more confident in every aspect of my life, including my writing.

I always enjoyed writing stories and poems from an early age, and in those early days without any fear of whether I was 'good enough' to call myself a writer. It is what I did and what I loved. I always dreamed of being like Jo from *Little Women*. Why then did I change my original path and pursue a career in law instead?

At some point in my childhood I remember my dad saying, "Nothing is worth doing if you don't do it well." To put it in context, he was talking about cleaning the wooden floor in our living room. He was dissatisfied with what he called my 'porthole cleaning'. As is the way with children, I took that on board as a message for how I should be in everything I did. In recent years I have learned a little about mindfulness and similar practices, and come across the thinking of Eckhart Tolle. It has helped me conclude that in my subconscious I came up with the idea that 'I am a perfectionist' and nothing less than perfection was good enough.

Although I continued to enjoy writing throughout school and beyond, I recall thinking at the time when I had to make decisions about university, that I only wanted to be a writer if I knew I could do it brilliantly well. I wanted to write the sort of work I was studying in my English Literature classes. Nothing less would do. The writer I wanted to be was a future self. In the meantime I would pursue what I thought would be a more lucrative career to enable me to reach that future self.

In a nutshell, there was my stumbling block to becoming a writer: my past self that had defined me as a perfectionist, and my dream of an unattainable future self that had to be a prize winning literary novelist. In my subconscious I had convinced myself that I was not good enough to be a writer.

Fortunately, I have had my epiphany. A few years ago I attended a therapy session called *The Journey* (originated by Brandon Bays). It revealed to me for the first time this subconscious idea I had that 'I am not good enough'. It was an astonishing revelation to me, but it all made sense. In my rational adult head I knew that it was a nonsense idea, but just acknowledging this subconscious blocker meant I felt free to feel 'good enough' in many aspects of my life. In my writing in particular, it gave me the confidence to join a writing course. I never imagined that over three years later it would remain a regular part of my life. I never before imagined having the confidence to read my work out to other writers.

Letting go of perfectionism has taken a little longer. For someone to want to pay for my work, it would have to be perfect wouldn't it? Of course 'perfection' is unattainable. Everything can always be improved upon. Every artist has to reach a point where they put their name on the canvas. Every author has to reach a point where they put down their pen and send their work off for consideration. One of the law partners I worked for once said that the document I was drafting didn't need to be perfect. The client didn't need something which was perfect, they just needed it to work. Of course, back then, I didn't agree. I didn't see how it could work if it was not perfect. Nothing is 'perfect' in that sense though. An orange is more or less a sphere, but it is not a perfect sphere. Every orange is different, but it works as an orange, and its imperfection is what makes it beautiful and interesting.

To anyone who has a longing to write but is somehow afraid to, I recommend you get your head in the right place as soon as possible. Find out what is causing your blockers and free yourself to follow your dream. Always remember we are all perfectly imperfect. Live in the present and, don't worry about it, just write and enjoy it.

Recommended reading:
Becoming a Writer - Dorothea Brande
The Power of Now - Eckhart Tolle

ARRAN'S STANDING STONES

Clair Wright

Wind whips grassy waves
Skylark trails spirals of song
Tall stones slice the sun

The sky darkens over the mountains to the north, but to our left, in the east, the sea sparkles. A strong wind buffets us as we tramp over the coarse tussocks of marsh grass. Oliver's small hand is warm in mine; he pushes his face into his coat, retreating from the cold. William runs ahead, excited by the sense of discovery. The grass ripples in a golden ocean, William's red coat billows like a spinnaker. Our ears ache with the incessant wind.

We startle a skylark, and it explodes into indignant song, climbing in jerky, breathless bursts high into the vivid blue sky. We reach the first stone circle and crouch behind the largest stones, taking a moment's rest from the wind's onslaught. Concentric rings of rounded grey boulders nestle in the rough grass, with gaps here and there like missing teeth.

Respite over, we continue across the exposed curve of the moor towards the standing stones. They punctuate the land, slicing through the grass and reaching towards the sky. Crisp shadows spring out where they meet the earth.

The little hand slips from mine and the boys run together, stumbling as their feet catch in the bracken. They reach the stones and their excited cries carry back to us on the wind. They run between the stones, flattening their bodies against them, pressing palms and cheeks into their pitted flanks.

"Why are they here?" they ask.

The wind whips our hair into our faces. The clouds hang heavy over the mountains. The skylarks sing regardless into the blue sky. The stones stand on the moor, defying four millennia.

They are the question, and the answer.

CHOOSE DAY

Suzanne Hudson

I wake up on Tuesdays and for a split second I have to remind myself what day it is, as I do every morning. But on Tuesdays I lie in bed and grin broadly. I feel my heart skip with excitement. It's Tuesday, or as I like to call it, *Choose Day*.

Tuesdays are my day when I do exactly as I choose. Once the children are deposited at school, I drive to my creative writing class which lasts from 10 am until midday. I then walk to a café where I join the other members of the Yorkshire Writers' Lunch. We spend a couple of hours sharing our latest work and talking about writing and then it's time to drive home to pick up the children.

I work part-time as a supply teacher and I had got into the habit of taking an afternoon's work on a Tuesday sometimes, but I recently decided that it was time to protect this day. For the rest of the week, any time for writing is squeezed in between working, looking after my children, cooking, cleaning and the general demands of everyday life. But for these few hours on a Tuesday, I can devote myself entirely to the art of writing. I sit in my writing class and luxuriate in simply being there. I know that this time tomorrow, I will be teaching a class of thirty children, so these precious hours feel like a gift.

I need this one day a week when I am nobody's wife, mother or teacher, I am just me. As a mother, you can easily lose your identity. You can forget who you are. Even in these enlightened times, taking time for yourself can bring on pangs of guilt. But I know that following my passion makes me a better wife, mother and teacher. I come home on Tuesdays happy, revitalised and better able to cope with the rest of my week.

I also delight in the fact that my children are now beginning to see me as a writer. I recently had an article published in the *Times Educational Supplement* which started life as a piece of homework for my writing class. I squealed when I saw it in print and my children cheered with me. I realised then that I was sending them an important message. Not only that I am a person in my own right, but that *they* can achieve their dreams, too.

EXAM NERVES

Emma Harding

"Turn over your papers now."

My palms are sweaty as I reach for the bundle of pages in front of me. The butterflies in my stomach have turned into dragons, breathing fire. I stare at the text but it could be written in Egyptian for all the sense it makes. I squeeze my eyes tight shut hoping that when I open them all will become clear. A deep breath, then open.

For a moment I'm blinded by light, then as my eyes adjust I can see the exam paper but it's moving away from me. I stretch out but the papers and the desk they're on recede from my touch. Then I realise it's not them that's moving, it's me. I'm drifting upwards. Below me are the rows of desks and students. No one seems to have noticed what's happening to me. I call out but there is no response. I look for my desk but there are no empty places. Is that me down there? I've never seen the top of my head before. There's no doubt it's me though - mousey-brown hair tied back in a ponytail and lime green fingernails. Is this an out-of-body experience? How about that?

I bump gently into the ceiling like a loose helium balloon. The people below me look small and still, a regimented army doing battle with GCSE English. On the floor beneath them are the lines and patterns of different sports - green for netball, blue for badminton and tennis, yellow for indoor footy. At this level I can see through the high gymnasium windows out onto the sports field.

There's a game of hockey in motion, white-shirted players moving swiftly from one side of the pitch to the other, their sticks outstretched. Mr Potts, the P.E. teacher, places his whistle in his mouth and points at a player. I can't hear anything though. It's silent in here apart from the whisper of pages being turned and the occasional muffled cough.

I push against the ceiling and begin to drift downwards. It's a bit like swimming. I approximate a front crawl motion and find I can control the direction and speed of travel. I float over to where Mr Jennings is sat facing the pupils. He's supposed to be invigilating but appears to be engrossed in a book. I lower myself to just above his head. I can see the shine of his bald spot and flakes of dandruff on his shoulders. What's he reading? The cover says *Pride and Prejudice* but the contents don't look like anything Jane Austen would write. It's more like *Shades of Grey*. Mr Jennings! Who knew you were such a perv?

A thought occurs. If I can read the teacher's book over his shoulder then maybe …? I do a sort of breaststroke and swim away from Mr Jennings towards the middle of the room. Here she is. Amanda, head bowed, pen moving at speed across the page. She's such a goody-goody. First to put her hand up, first with an A*. She might just be my saviour. I peer down at her writing, words streaming out behind her pen. It's like a blue ribbon, a swirl of letters and words, as meaningless as the hieroglyphics on my exam papers. Then I notice a similar swirl of ink on the palm of her other hand and on her wrist and disappearing under her sleeve. Amanda Phillips, you dirty cheat!

Mr Jennings is on the move. He walks down the central aisle towards me. I mean towards the actual me, sitting at my desk with my eyes closed. I watch from above. He leans over my desk and says in an exaggerated whisper, "Time to wake up, young lady. Clock's ticking." I open my eyes and I'm there sat at my desk looking at Mr Jennings in the face, his stale cigarette breath filling my nostrils. He frowns, stabs his finger at the paper before me as if I've forgotten what we're here for. Then he straightens and walks away.

I look down at the first question on the paper, and heave a sigh of relief as the letters and words resolve themselves into legibility. I read it carefully.

'Describe how Jane Austen uses bird's eye view narration to reveal unexpected insights into the characters in *Pride and Prejudice.*'

You've gotta be kidding me.

THE BUTTERFLY BROOCH

Suzanne Hudson

Danny said let's go out tonight, but
I didn't want to. My best dress was getting
Shabby and the holes in the bottom
Of my shoes would show when we jived
Together.

He pleaded and said are you still
Sulking about your Mam's butterfly brooch?
Pride got the better of me. I would never
Let him know that I crossed the road on
Lake Street now, so as not to see it in the
Pawnbroker's window.

My hand shook when I handed it over
To Mr Levenstein and he had to
Uncurl my fingers one by one to
Release my grip. He licked his lips and
I wanted to be sick.

Danny said it was just 'til he got
Paid what he was owed and then
I could get it back. Another week and the
Landlord would throw us out, was that what I
Wanted? No, I said, but I vowed silently that
I'd never let it go again.

There's a little left over, Danny said, so
Let's have a night of dancing and
Forget our troubles, shall we?
I wanted him to swing me around and
Remember what it felt like
To be young and carefree.

She saw me coming in and
Turned away, doing that
Fake laugh with her cronies
That says Look at me! I'm so pretty
And popular and so much better than you.

Belinda James had always been the
Queen Bee around here. Mam used to say she
Was pure evil and wasn't her mother
Just the same? I tried not to notice her
New, lemon-yellow dress and freshly-
Starched petticoats.

Danny got me a lager shandy and I drank
It far too fast. I could see something glinting
In the mirror behind the bar and I turned to see
Her there before me, her bosom in my face
And my butterfly brooch nestled in her cleavage.

I ripped it from her dress with such
Might that the satin tore right down the
Middle and she fell backwards in slow motion
Onto the sticky floor, her brassiere's stiff peaks
Pointing to the ceiling,

Exposed for all to see.
I gasped.
The music stopped. A hush
Came over the dance hall. A hundred faces watched
Us, waiting.

And then the clapping started. Quiet at first, then
It rippled around the room, gathering momentum.
No one helped her up. She screamed at her cronies
And they turned away. Shc tried to get up and she
Slipped on the beer-drenched floor.

Then the laughter started
And the jeers and stamping.
Her face burned a deep crimson. She stumbled
To her feet and fled, firing swear words at us that we
Didn't know she knew.

The band struck up. I pinned on my butterfly brooch and
Danny swung me around and
Threw me up in the air,
Just as he did when
We were young and carefree.

THE JOY OF WRITING

Virginia Hainsworth

I searched for inspiration
but nothing could I find.
I trawled my tired and fuddled brain,
every quadrant of my mind.

I tried in vain to mind map
but my writing pad stayed blank.
Perhaps some soothing music would help
but into a doze I sank.

So next, I thought I'd meditate.
Maybe help would come.
I sat on the floor and closed my eyes,
Contemplated 'til my bum was numb.

But still no muse, no creative ideas
entered my empty head.
So I thought I'd completely distract myself
and take a bath instead.

One hour later, back I came,
with wrinkled fingers and toes.
Warm, relaxed and clean was I,
pen poised, still nothing shows.

And then I turned to alcohol
to try to free my head.
Purely in the pursuit of art, you know,
I emptied a bottle of red.

Frustrated, disheartened, fed up I became
and so I deserted my pen.
I resorted to cleaning 'neath the kitchen sink
and tidying the den.

I washed my mascara brush, of course,
and polished the kettle as well
but still I could think of nothing to write
and then, in my head, rang a bell.

I could write about writing nothing at all!
And, in a flash, this poem came.
So, if you're not smart or creative today,
you could always try the mundane!

SEAFOOD PLATTER

taste the sea with these fishy tales

THE FISH MARKET

Emma Harding

It's busy. Crowds of people mill about, some purposeful, others standing in groups, deep in conversation. The natives are dressed in dark warm clothes, the odd tourist standing out like a sore thumb in brightly coloured t-shirt, shorts and sandals. Seagulls shriek impatiently overhead. Small trestle tables line up along each side of the jetty, some shaded from the sun with striped umbrellas. Against the seaward side, fishing boats bob and rock in gentle rhythm, resting after a long night's toil.

For the fishermen, there's still work to be done. They are here to sell. Each has laid out his stall with his catch and there's a huge variety on display.

Some major in shellfish, piles of blue-black *cozze*, delicate pale grey *vongole* and the Sicilian speciality, *gamberi rosso,* vermillion and translucent. Others have landed multitudes of small silver fish, slender *sarde*, metallic *orato*, curled into stiff bracelets, and slivers of *acciughe*, all ripe for dishes of *fritto misto*. On other stalls, there are alien-looking *polpi*, their tentacles coiled together in a glossy mass, and prettily speckled *calamari*. The biggest stalls display great tranches of flesh, blood-red *tonno* and *pesce spada*.

One stall-holder, big and tired, his face raddled by sun and sea-water, shakes a shower of ice over his catch. Another shouts his wares, a cigarette in one hand, both hands gesticulating in the direction of a trio of women at the next table. The woman closest to him, without looking, raises her arm in a gesture of impatience or dismissal. He shrugs and turns his attention to another group on his left. On another stall, a transaction is underway. Great handfuls of anchovies are dropped into a plastic bag and weighed using old-fashioned weights and scales. All the while, trader and customer engage in an energetic conversation about who-knows-what - the price of fish? The politics of the day? A family upset? Then money changes hands, hands are shaken and a *"grazie, ciao"* exchanged.

FOOTWEAR

Dave Rigby

From a seat by the window I can see the restless grey lake. A boat moves jerkily out of view propelled by inexpert rowers anxious to reach the deserted jetty.

Heels click on the quarry-tiled floor, black, highly polished, tightly-laced shoes, the waiter making his presence known, the showman displaying his on-stage skills.

He tells me I shouldn't miss the fish chowder. I nod and add my obligatory Americano with cold milk. His metallic studs recede; the swing door barely slows his determined progress through to the steam-filled kitchen.

Silver boots with small heels emerge, tray balanced with accustomed ease on outstretched hand, teapot, milk jug, cups, saucers, scones, jam, cream eagerly awaited at table six. The two women exchange cruise stories in gradually rising voices. A brief silence whilst crockery is organised, milk and tea poured, sugar spooned, scones cut and spread. Then tales of disembarking at Venice continue.

The waitress glances momentarily at her silver boots as they make their confident way back to the kitchen. The door swings again.

I shuffle my feet to ease off well-worn walking boots surreptitiously and edge them under the table. I continue with my lack of progress on twenty-three down and think of fish.

Brown shoes with long, long pointed toecaps emerge

from behind the counter. A surprise choice for the balding, older man who moves slowly across the café, his long apron flapping, to clear table ten. Well – a surprise for me, but probably not for him.

There is no sign yet of my steaming chowder bowl, or the answer to twenty-three down. The wind whips across the distant lake and trees sway in expertly choreographed unison. I push my boots closer to the warmth of the radiator, where they're joined by black and red striped feet.

A familiar click, click announces the arrival of coffee. "Make that two fish chowders," I tell him as, at last, rainbow coloured wellington boots cross the floor, toes turned slightly inwards, trailing wet, mud-tinged, puddles.

She lowers her tall frame on to the chair opposite and smiles that smile.

MAIN COURSES

hearty reads to get your teeth into and
some serious food for thought

THE LUNCHEON PARTY

Suzanne Hudson

"So it's just a little luncheon party..." Simone was saying and Claudette's eyes were glazing over, in the way they always did when her friend regaled her with the long list of social events that she was going to or hosting. Claudette sipped her red wine and thought about the painting she was working on. Just hearing about Simone's hectic social plans made her feel exhausted.

That's another reason I didn't marry, she thought to herself. The endless parties and suppers and entertaining would have bored her rigid. A film producer's wife, Simone had happily immersed herself into Parisian society and it was all her old school friend seemed to talk about these days. Claudette was a painter, a free spirit and a solitary animal. She liked nothing better than dining alone in a restaurant with a good book for a companion. People drained her energy and small talk paralysed her. She smiled her best non-committal smile while Simone chattered on about the menu, her new sequinned flapper dress and the guest list.

"And then there's someone else that you know, or used to know."

"Oh yes, who's that?" Claudette asked, barely caring as she had already made up her mind that she was busy that day.

"Phillippe."

Claudette's heart leapt into her mouth.

"Phillippe Dupont?"

"Yes, that's right. He's home from America for a holiday. He's just made his first movie. He's tipped for stardom, Henri says."

A memory flashed through Claudette's mind. The summer house in Simone's country home. Tennis whites, grass stains and sunburn. Champagne going to her head, making the stuffy room spin. A bee buzzing at the window as Phillippe held her in his arms, his lips caressing her neck, his hand moving up her bare thigh.

"So you'll come?" Simone's question punctured her daydream.

"I'd love to," she said, trying to hide her delight, to stifle the huge grin that had spread across her face. She saw Simone frown, just a little, in surprise.

"I didn't know if you'd remember him…"

"Oh yes I do," Claudette said, realising to her horror that a blush was spreading over her cheeks. Seeing her friend's look of interest, she muttered, "Well, vaguely. So when's this luncheon?"

"Sunday the 18th. Drinks on the terrace from noon."

Claudette reached into her handbag for her slim leather diary and began flicking through the empty pages. She felt Simone's eyes on her as she found the date and scribbled in the details with a pencil. She knew she was grinning like a fool, but she couldn't help it. Her heart was singing. Phillippe! Wonderful, handsome, funny Phillippe, who lit up any room he was in. It was five years since he'd left. She'd thought she'd never see him again.

"Of course he's married now," Simone said, and Claudette thought she heard a gentle warning in her friend's voice.

"Of course!" she smiled, her heart sinking slightly.

"But he's travelling alone as his wife is expecting their first baby."

"How lovely!"

"We'd love for you to come, but if you're too busy, please don't worry darling. I know these things aren't your scene."

Their eyes met for a second. Claudette held up her blank diary for her friend to see.

"Busy? I don't think so, my dear! It will be fun. You keep telling me I need to get out more."

"Mmm. I just don't want you to be bored, that's all."

"Oh there's no danger of that."

***

He'd asked her to go to the States with him. Practically begged her. He said he wouldn't be coming back. Broadway was calling him. They lay in bed in his apartment as the sun came up over the river and he described the art scene in New York and how wonderful it would be for her career. He said that they could get married first if it made her feel better and she laughed and told him that was an appalling way to propose and she wasn't the marrying kind. She said that she couldn't leave France, her family, her friends. Her grandmother had always said that a woman should never follow a man anywhere, that it should always be the other way around. He said he loved her, that he couldn't bear to be apart from her and if that was the case then he wouldn't leave, there was plenty of acting work for him here in Paris.

She knew that he must really love her to give up his dreams. So when they met for dinner that evening she'd made up her mind to move to America with him. She thought she'd burst with excitement while the waiter took their order and Phillippe deliberated between fish and steak. As the waiter walked away, she grabbed both his hands.

"I've got something to tell you," she said, her eyes sparkling with happiness. His face looked grave.

"Before you say anything, I've got something I must tell you," he said. She opened her mouth to protest and then saw in his eyes that he was about to break her heart.

"I'm sorry my darling, I've been thinking about it all day. I know I said this morning that I would stay here, but I can't. I have to leave, I really believe that great things are going to happen for me in New York. Please forgive me but I cannot give up this chance to live my dream. Perhaps one day you will change your mind and join me there?"

She let go of his hands.

"So what was it you wanted to tell me?"

"Oh, it's nothing," she murmured, as the waiter poured her wine.

She cried for two days straight when he left. And she didn't paint for three weeks. When she did pick up her brush her paintings were red and black and angry. But time healed her wounds. Other men flitted in and out of her life, but none of them seemed quite right. She gradually forgave him and she never forgot him. He was true to his word, he never came home. Until now.

***

After Simone's invitation that day at the café, she found she couldn't stop thinking about Phillippe. She abandoned her landscapes and began painting him. The back of his head. A side profile. In the distance coming towards her. She felt like she'd lost her mind. She thought she saw him on the street buying a newspaper, on the metro, at the cinema. She ran behind him for half a block to grab the shoulder of a complete stranger, who looked at her with horror. She dreamt that they were in New York, that she had married him, that she was heavily pregnant. I'm going to France for a holiday, he was saying, and she was hanging onto his leg, screaming hysterically, don't go, don't go. She awoke in a cold sweat and felt her flat stomach beneath her nightgown and for a horrifying split second thought she'd lost his baby.

The day of the luncheon party arrived. Claudette dressed with shaking hands. A fantasy was running through her head. He was divorcing his wife. He'd found out the baby wasn't his. He wasn't really home for a holiday. He had realised that he had made the greatest mistake of his life five years ago and he wanted a second chance. As she applied her make-up, she rehearsed her responses. No, he couldn't just snap his fingers and expect her to take him back. It was too late. She'd moved on. She didn't love him anymore. But her fantasy always ended in him grabbing her and kissing her and her falling under his spell all over again.

Simone's butler opened the front door and took Claudette's wrap. Simone greeted her in the hallway, exclaiming over her silver dress and beaded headband. She swept her off through the house to the terrace. Claudette's eyes scanned the room, her heart pounding. Simone squeezed her hand.

"He's over there," she said, nodding towards the corner of the terrace where a tall dark-haired man had his back to them and was holding court to a gaggle of beautiful young women.

"He's not changed," Simone whispered. "Always an eye for the ladies."

"Really?" Claudette asked, wondering what her friend meant.

"You're not under the illusion that you were the only one, are you?" Simone asked, gently.

Claudette laughed, "Of course not," and steadied herself by holding the back of a chair.

"He's slept with half the women in this room. Including me."

"I see." She felt herself gasping for air.

Peals of laughter emanated from the group in the corner.

"Henri doesn't know of course. He likes to kid himself that I was a virgin when we married."

"Simone, I'm sorry, this was a mistake. I think it might be best if I go."

"Are you sure?"

"I'm certain. Thank you, my darling, but you know I hate this kind of thing."

Simone's butler hailed her a cab and as Claudette sank into the back of it, the tears came. Tears of anger, tears of regret. She'd always imagined him pining for her, kicking himself for leaving her behind five years ago. And a tiny part of her always thought he'd come back for her one day.

Later that month she packed up to leave for London. She realised that one of the reasons she'd never left Paris was so that Phillippe would always know where to find her. As she stored away her paintings she came across the one of the back of his head. She decided to take it with her. To remind her to always let go of the ones who walk away.

ORK

Dave Rigby

Ork can hear something out there in the pitch black night, some noise behind the buffeting of the wind in the eaves. The bed is almost warm. Reluctantly he heaves off the blankets and walks in his bed-socks to the window, pulling back a corner of the heavy curtains. He is rewarded with a view of complete darkness, not even a twinkle of light to be seen. He hears the sound again, an unpleasant sound.

He returns to the already cold bed, lies on his back, covers up to his chin and tries to forget.

At first light he is awake again. He dresses and descends the steep stairs to the kitchen. He pulls back the heavy oak door and peers out into the yard. The crow is clearly dead. It's not the first time, but he still doesn't know the meaning of these messages.

He fills the wooden pail, moving the pump handle vigorously, watching the live crows circling the beech copse on the hillside. The axe is newly sharpened and he's able to split the logs with minimal effort, storing them in the large wicker basket by the range.

The bread is stale but it's all he has and he spreads the almost rancid butter thinly as he watches the kettle come to the boil. The precious coffee is eked out – one small miserly spoonful. He breathes in the smell greedily as he waits for it to brew. The egg sits on the saucer, large, brown, covered in shit and straw. Should he eat it now or save it? He decides to abstain. He chews slowly, planning the day's work and thinking of his wife. How long is it now – a month?

Victor is pleased to see him and Digger fusses around his feet, tail wagging. Mounted up, Ork allows the horse to find its way along the stony track at a gentle pace towards the town. The trees are in early leaf, an almost blinding green. Occasional gusts of wind, the remains of the overnight storm, blow raindrops from the branches above, onto the passing trio. As they reach the top of the ridge he sees the town spread out beneath, smoke curling from chimneys, the river sparkling in the intermittent sunshine. He can just pick out the men on the bridge, armed men dressed in dark coats. Ork knows he will need to be careful with his work today, more careful than usual.

He stables Victor and looks into the horse's eyes for a few moments. Digger waits patiently. Ork unlocks the door to the printing room and knows immediately that someone has been there overnight.

***

Ork walks around the printing room slowly and takes in the mess of papers on the long trestle table and the unfamiliar boot marks on the flagstone that never dries. The cupboard is still locked and he breathes a sigh of relief.

There's a knock at the door. He's surprised to find a customer who wants to pay him. As he prepares the press for the day's work, Ork thinks of the provisions he'll be able to buy. An image of a foaming pewter tankard floats in front of him. All in good time he thinks.

When he finally takes out his pocket watch, he can't believe the day has gone. His hunger hits him suddenly. He wipes his ink-stained fingers on an already blackened cloth and walks to the door, Digger at his heels. The Oak provides a welcome refuge. He spreads the newspaper on the table, drinks from the tankard and chews the mutton slowly. He reads about the latest Treason Trial. The Government is running scared, Habeus Corpus suspended.

The last mouthful gone, he pushes back his chair, crosses his legs and lights his pipe. Its smoke curls towards the log-filled hearth and is lost in the flames. Ork feels almost contented. Jonas joins him silently and picks up the newspaper, studying it intently. He tells Ork the cart is ready.

Under cover of darkness, they retreat to the print room. They work in the dim candlelight, beneath the shuttered windows, the regular rhythm of the machine almost hypnotic. Ork scans the first of the printed tracts looking for mistakes that he knows aren't there. It reads well enough. Thomas Paine himself would be pleased. The pamphlets are wrapped carefully, each bundle tied tightly with twine. Jonas opens the connecting door to the stable and harnesses Victor who stands patiently between the shafts of the cart. Once the bundles have been loaded, Ork secures them under the tarpaulin. The two men shake hands. Ork opens the stable doors and watches as horse, cart and man disappear into the night.

The walk home is long and cold, the knapsack heavy. As he nears his house, he hears the sound of footsteps. Dropping to his knees and restraining the dog, he watches and listens. He sees a figure moving towards the stable, a shape dangling from his hand. A word from Ork sets Digger off towards his victim.

The dead crow drops to the ground as the intruder falls forward. Ork drags the man inside the stable, binds his wrists and tethers him loosely to the stall. Only when he lights the lamp does he realise it's his apprentice – his former apprentice, still a lad in all but height.

***

Ork's sleep is undisturbed. In the daylight he notices the envelope wedged under a stone by the back door. Bacon and egg, coffee and bread. What it is to have some money. Breakfast completed, he stares for a while at the unmarked envelope propped against the candlestick, before slitting it carefully and pulling out a single thin sheet of paper. He recognises his wife's hand immediately and wonders how she has managed to get the letter to him. A shout from the stable reminds him of his own prisoner and his relief that the crow warnings were nothing more sinister than youthful revenge.

As he crosses the yard, a movement on the hillside catches his eye. For a moment he thinks it might be Jonas returning, but there are two of them and he can see their muskets glinting in the early morning sunlight.

The horses slip and slide down the wet hillside towards Ork's house.

The two men dismount unhurriedly. Ork watches them carefully, uncertain of what he can do to save himself, if they have harmful intent. They keep their distance and the taller man speaks in a strange accent which Ork fails to recognise. He has to ask the man to repeat his question.

"I am Ork. I am the printer." He sees no point in denying it. "How do you want me to help you?" He addresses the taller man, but it is the short squat man who answers.

"You misunderstand. It is we who can help you." His face twitches as he hears a shout from the shed and Ork quickly explains about the sins of his former apprentice. "Perhaps it would be better if your sinner doesn't overhear our conversation. We shall leave now."

Riding two on a horse is never satisfactory – for men or horse. Digger runs between the two mounts, confused by Victor's absence. Ork's hunger hits him as they descend the wooded valley to the stone bridge. The cart is on its side, its precious cargo strewn across the river bank, no sign of Jonas or Victor.

The three men heave the cart back onto its wheels and laboriously load the pamphlets, bundle by bundle. Digger sniffs the churned mud, whines and pads slowly away to the trees.

The smaller man tells Ork he's lucky. Had they been staunch loyalists, he would have been on a treason charge. But he and his comrade have no truck with such out of date thinking.

"We must learn from the French. When we saw your over-turned wagon and stopped to read your handiwork, we knew we could count on you. You will of course want to come with us."

Ork takes in the speaker's subtle change of tone, an order not a request. He's come across their views before, but they are not his. He wonders how they were able to track him down and worries about Jonas' fate.

Digger's sudden barking distracts him. Ork walks into the copse, feeling the eyes of both men on his back, as they follow. He discovers Victor tethered to a birch sapling.

"That was well found. Bring him, he can pull the cart." Another order.

Ork guides the cart skilfully around the muddy morass and over the packhorse bridge. He follows his captors as they make their way east, smoking and jesting. Ork thinks of his wife's letter. Is there a chance she'll be freed shortly? He blames himself for her incarceration. If he hadn't been away from home that day…

The men hide their muskets under the tarpaulin, well out of his reach and take on an air of normality as they reach the edge of the town. Ork has seldom visited this place, but the men seem to know it well and are greeted by some of the townsfolk as they ride by.

Horse and cart enter the stable. Ork jumps down and is immediately seized by the two men and led to a room at the rear, dominated by a printing press.

"We have work for you to do," the smaller man says in a low voice.

It's only then Ork realises that Digger is missing.

***

At least they feed him. A hungry worker is a poor worker they tell him. Their tract is the work of traitors. Although Ork could never put his name to such a document, he has no choice but to use the press that will bring their tract to life. The machine has not been well treated and he curses at the frequent breakdowns. But his skills and his dextrous fingers come to his aid. He works all day and well into the evening.

His captors are pleased with his progress and tell him of

their future plans, how together they will make a forceful team. At last he is allowed to sleep, but without further food. He dreams of Digger by his side. Woken by cold and hunger, he rises in the darkness and feels his way around the room. He edges towards the single doorway which he finds locked and barred.

Did he imagine a ceiling hatch or was it really there? He moves carefully through the darkness to where his memory – or his imagination – tells him the hatch should be. The ceiling is almost twice the height of a man. He removes paper stacks from the table and drags it into position, making noises he is sure will awaken someone. But all is quiet. Standing on the table he is able to reach and hope. The rough wooden panel greets him and he pushes upwards. His arms, strong from years of labour, haul him up into the space beneath the roof, slipped slates revealing pinpricks of what must be moonlight. He feels his way carefully across the joists, crosses the top of a rubble-filled wall and continues. He concludes he must now be over a different room and searches for a second hatch. His luck holds. The board is tight-fitting and Ork struggles to prise it open, paying the price of broken nails and grazed fingers. Only as he's dropping to the floor below, does he see the dim outline of a sleeping figure and curses his sudden change in fortune.

The figure stirs and to prevent any cry of alarm, Ork moves swiftly to clap his large hand around the mouth of his captive. There is just enough light from a tiny window above the door for Ork to recognise that the man he is silencing is Jonas. Whispered greetings are followed by whispered explanations of capture and forced labour. Ork removes the bonds from his friend's hands and legs. Jonas leads them to a recess. He knows there are tools stored there and he selects a long metal bar which he uses to lever open the bolted door. At the sound of the timber jamb splintering, they freeze. But there is no sound of footsteps. They enter a wooden lean-to and Ork smells Victor before he sees him.

Saddled and reined, they lead the horse through the unlocked gate into the night air. At the end of the street, they both mount Victor and pass through the silent town.

The ride is long and hard. On the moonlit riverbank, they talk of the precautions to be taken, should their captors come visiting again, whilst Victor drinks and grazes. By the time they eventually descend the hill behind Ork's house, they are all exhausted. Ork is just alert enough to glimpse the weak candlelight flickering through the kitchen window. They dismount and he signals for Jonas to move to the front door, to block any escape, whilst he moves cautiously to the back door. He finds the entrance bolted. Peering through the window he sees the vague, shadowy outline of a woman. Whoever her few muffled words are addressed to, is out of sight.

When he sees Jonas enter the room, he shouts to warn him of the danger. As she hears Ork's voice, the woman turns to face the window. She smiles at her husband. Her previously hidden listener bounds into view, barking, tail wagging furiously.

THE DISAPPEARANCE

A collaborative experiment by Virginia Hainsworth, Andrew Shephard, Emma Harding, Clair Wright & Dave Rigby

Steven Fielding lives with his partner and her two young children in a Northern town close to the Pennines. He works long hours during the week and spends most of his weekends with his family. Steve was last seen (by a friend) three days ago, on a sunny May morning, boarding his usual 8.00am train. He's not responding to phone calls, texts or emails. He doesn't use Twitter or Facebook. Nobody can remember him going off the radar before. Apart from being a little overweight, he's generally in good health. His partner has informed the police that he is missing, but, so far, no evidence has emerged of any suspicious circumstances surrounding his sudden disappearance.

ELLIE

It's three o'clock in the morning. I am awake. Again. I gaze through the open curtains at the bare-faced moon. It is a delicate, dreamy blue and it stares back, unblinkingly, at me. I wish it could tell me where you are.

I turn to your empty pillow and hug it pathetically. Where are you? I know you are out there, somewhere, alive. I would sense it if you weren't.

I've told the children that you have gone away for a few days with work. I hate lying to them, but what can I do? Cassie asked if you had gone to stay with her dad.

For what must be the hundredth time, I trawl every

quadrant of my brain for anything unusual in the days leading up to Tuesday morning when you left for work, as normal. I've been over this so many times in my head and with the police. You left, as you always do, in a rush. You didn't take your wallet and bank cards. You never do. Just enough money for the day. I can never understand why you do that.

I'm afraid I've looked through all your papers in your desk drawer, to see if there is anything out of the ordinary. I'm sorry, but I just felt that I had to and, anyway, the police told me to search. I felt like a snoop. I couldn't find anything odd. Your passport wasn't there, of course, but we couldn't find it when we got back from holiday a couple of weeks ago. We thought you must have lost it coming out of the airport on the way home. Did you remember to report it missing? I bet you've forgotten. That's so like you.

It's past four o'clock now. The moon is dipping down behind the houses at the back. Just peeping over the chimney pots. It's teasing me. It's taunting me with the thought that you may have left me for someone else. I know you haven't, but the police referred to the possibility. As did your mother. She asked if everything was alright "between the two of you, if you know what I mean." As if I would tell her if there was anything wrong. She wants to come and stay but I just couldn't cope with that. Part of me feels bad about saying no because she must be feeling pretty wretched. The sliding moon has another disquieting thought for me as it slinks down even lower. Your mother seemed a bit evasive when we spoke today. Hesitant. I try to cancel that thought. She always sounds cagey with me.

And your closest friend, Jim. Have you confided anything in him? He said not. No, you wouldn't, would you? You wouldn't tell Jim anything you hadn't told me. Not Jim, of all people.

It's five a.m now and the guilty moon has disappeared completely, leaving me feeling even more alone. I must have slept a little, because remnants of a dream claw at my mind. You in a dark place. You're calling my name, but it's not my name you're calling. It's my old name. The one you don't know about, the one you can't possibly know, can never know. I'm back in the children's home, where I grew up. The one I told you about. Then I can hear my mother calling me, the mother I never knew. But I can't hear what name she's using. Her voice turns into yours. You're in a sunless place. Your voice grows fainter and more fragile. It disappears completely as I become fully awake.

Six a.m now and the sun is well over the horizon, sweeping into the corners of my mind and casting away all shadowy thoughts. For the time being at least.

I am left with the certain knowledge that you must be ill. Certain, that is, until the next thought. You're ill. That can be the only explanation. I'm sorry I didn't realise. Can you forgive me for not noticing? I'll come and find you. I'll bring you home and look after you. I'll help you to get better. No one need know you're ill. I feel as though I should know where you are.

I suddenly notice the faint outline of the moon. It hasn't gone after all.

JIM

Every time my mind races ahead I pinch myself hard. *Stay calm, Jimmy Boy, stay calm.* The important thing is to act normal, do nothing unusual. They know that in the films, but then they do something stupid that gives them away.

She rang me, Ellie did. She's never rung me before. That's how good she is at hiding her feelings. I was half way down the High Street on my morning trip to look at the runners and riders in Ladbrokes. Ellie said she needed to talk to me.

"Sure, Babe. Talk away." I bobbed into a coffee shop and mouthed *espresso* to the barista. My heart was thumping. It was the call I'd been waiting for.

"It's Steven. I'm worried sick, Jim. Have you seen him?" She really did sound worried. She didn't even bother to tell me not to call her 'Babe'.

"Seen him? When d'you mean?"

"I mean he left for work yesterday morning and hasn't been home. I told the police and they asked if I'd checked with all his friends." She sounded really stressed. *The police;* was that a warning?

"Hold on, I need to pay for the coffee." I needed a minute to work out the right answer. Had I seen Steve? Did she want me to say I'd seen him?

"No. I waited for him in the Head of Steam last night but he didn't show."

"Is he in trouble, Jim? You must tell me. Does he owe someone money?" I had to stifle a laugh. Owe money? I was the one who owed Steve money. He was always helping me out, like a good old friend should.

"Jim, promise me. I mean this. If he contacts you let me know, right away. You must."

"I will, I promise. You know I will. I'd do anything for you."

I'd do anything for you. Was that giving too much away? What if the police were actually listening? *Be cool, Jimmy Boy*. I think she started to cry.

"Don't worry, love. He's probably got some business to attend to. He'll turn up in a day or two. I'll ask around if anyone's seen him. Are you all right on your own with the kids? Do you want me to come round?"

"No, Jim. I'm fine. I just want to know where he is."

I took my coffee outside and rolled a cigarette. I wondered how long I'd have to wait before it wouldn't look suspicious. A month? Six months? I'd already been waiting two years. Two years of hiding our feelings for each other. Two years of hanging around with Steve so I would have an excuse to see Ellie every few days. She played her part, never betraying the buzz we both felt when we were in the same room. She even blamed me for Steve's gambling and I went along with it, persuading Steve to lend me money so I had another reason to go round to their house.

Another six months of waiting would be hard. I will leave it to Ellie. She seems to have handled everything good enough up to now. She'll give me a sign. How will she let me know it's time? A kiss, as long and full on as all those kisses I've imagined? Or will she fall sobbing with relief into my arms? Or will it be that smouldering look she gave me the first time we met? I had just moved back into town and bumped into Steve when he was coming out of the station. He invited me home for a meal and to catch up on the last five years. It was late, and we were talking about people Ellie didn't know. She yawned, said she was going to bed, and smiled over her shoulder at me as she was climbing the stairs.

A look that said it all.

MRS FIELDING

So you've left. I can't say I'm all that surprised. You never seemed able to fully commit to life. To all its responsibilities. To all its difficulties. To everything you owed to people.

Eleanor called to let me know. Yes, I know. *Ellie* called to tell me you'd gone. She can't even use her actual name, that one. What do ... did ... you see in her? With her dodgy ex-husband and her scruffy children. She can't even give them proper names. What sort of name is 'Cassie' for goodness sake? Cassandra is such a beautiful name. A Greek goddess, I think. Was she the one who could predict the future but no one ever believed her?

Did you tell her? Ellie? She didn't say anything about it on the phone but I think I should go and see her. Look her in the eyes. Only then will I know if she knows.

I visited your father yesterday. To tell him the news. There were signs you had been there recently. Was that before you left or after? I talked to him about you but he was no more help than he had been when he was alive. Always one for retreating into silence at the first sign of trouble. Then, as now, I suppose.

He'd know what to say to you though. You always had

your heads together, you two. Plotting some scheme or trip together. You never shared any of that with me. I used to hate it, you know, being left out like that. Now I miss it. Now I'd give anything to be able to walk into the room and find you both there smirking guiltily at each other. Anything.

My head is full of 'if onlys'. Regrets that I can't shake off. If only you'd finished your degree. You were intelligent enough. You could have been anything you wanted. I worked so hard to get you there, made so many sacrifices. But you frittered it away, shrugged it off as if it meant nothing to you. I had such dreams for you. Where did all that promise go? I used to watch you as a child, envying your energy, your delight in new things, new experiences. The way you would drink in life. But somewhere along the line you got scared. You refused to push yourself. If you had you could be a doctor by now, earning a good salary, living in a big house. That's what I wanted for you. But instead you're in a dead-end job, with a dead-end 'wife'.

If only you'd stayed with Rebecca. Not Becky, never Becky. Beautiful, refined Rebecca. She had enough drive for both of you. She'd have made you what you should have been. She'd have given you children of your own. You would have been happy then. Settled.

If only your father were still alive. Yes I know what you said. That I was glad to be rid of him. I haven't seen you since the day you said those awful things. I swore I'd wait for you to apologise. But you haven't been back and now maybe you never will.

If only you hadn't found those things. I'm sorry about that. You weren't meant to. I meant to throw them out but somehow I couldn't bring myself to do it. But it's not what you thought. I tried to explain but you wouldn't listen. You said such horrible things to me. I thought I'd let you stew for a bit and then I'd explain. Now, maybe I won't get the chance. I loved your father you know. I couldn't bear seeing him in so much pain.

There's something I want you to know, wherever you are. I want you to know that your dad smiled at the end. He knew. And I knew. It was the right thing to do.

SARAH

I didn't think I would ever see you again. Not after all this time. I thought you'd left me, and all this, behind you. What made you come? Why now? Funny that you knew I would still be at the flat, our flat. Did you know I wouldn't move on? Not like you, Steven. You, with your nice job, nice home, nice life – all very settled, all very safe. Is that why you came? Is it all getting a bit boring for you?

Did you want a reminder of the old life, the old you? Was it strange to be sitting in our old flat, on our old sofa? It hasn't changed much; there's still a bit of damp in the corner of the bedroom, the tap still drips in the bathroom. I keep it tidier now, of course. But then, I'm not smoking as much as we were then.

It was nice to see you. You looked different - fatter, comfortable in your cord trousers and your chain store jumper. You look like a father, a family man. Are you a father, Steven? You didn't say, and I didn't want to ask.

You seemed sad though, Steven. Are you sad? Is that why you came? I wanted to reach out, to touch you, to kiss you again, but I was too afraid that you would push me away. You seemed to be on the edge of something, and I didn't want to push you, one way or the other.

You didn't tell me anything about your life now. I think you're with someone, maybe you're even married. Why didn't you want to tell me? Do you talk about your old life, with her? Do you talk about me? Or do you want to pretend you've always lived like you do now, a neat and tidy life, without chaos round every corner?

I bet your mum's proud of you now. You always wanted to put on a show for her. You never let her visit the flat, kept her away from the overflowing ashtrays, and the empty wine bottles. You would go home for the weekend, in your one shirt, and come back angry and silent, to roll another joint and fall into bed, with me. She must be pleased that you've settled down, that you're living the kind of life she approves of.

But we used to laugh at those people, didn't we Steven? Those dull-eyed zombies getting on the same train every day, to their dull jobs, then home again to their dull lives. It wasn't what we wanted for us. We wanted to do it differently.

Don't get me wrong. I admire you. You did well, straightening yourself out. I sometimes wish I could have done the same. Maybe then there would have been a future for us, together.

We were happy, weren't we? Looking back at that year, it's all a blur, a haze of smoke and red wine and sharing a line on my birthday, a fog of fighting and crying and making up again. We couldn't have carried on forever like that; we would have ended up as middle-aged dope-heads, or worse. It always had to end, one way or the other. Maybe the two of us together were like the stuff we were experimenting with; always on the edge of being toxic.

I wanted to tell you how much I've missed you, even now, after so long. I wanted to tell you how much I loved you. I still think about you, Steven. Is that why you came?

I always thought we would be together, in the end. I never thought you would leave me. I couldn't believe it when you'd gone. I waited for you to come back, for days. I just sat in the flat, and smoked and waited.

And then, after all this time, you came back. And you said you would come again, that you'd call me, but you haven't, yet. Did you have second thoughts? Did it scare you, seeing me again?

I hope you're okay, that you're happy, wherever you are.

STEVEN

"It's time for me to move on – again - Dad!" I remove the dying flowers from the vase and replace them with a fresh, petrol-station bunch. The display looks a bit thin so I pinch one or two extra blooms from nearby graves.

"That looks better. They'll never miss them." I reach for a ready-made roll-up. I know as a regular smoker, Dad won't mind. And like me it wasn't just tobacco he inhaled.

"I went down to see Sarah, to sort of say goodbye. Had my old clothes on – well she wouldn't be used to seeing me in a suit. She hasn't changed, offered me a spliff and was surprised when I refused. To be honest we didn't really have much to talk about. I can't believe we spent a whole year together –till I moved back north. Still she was good for me. I'd just been released and she helped me get things back together. So different from the saintly Rebecca – Mum's favourite, although I'm not sure you ever really liked her." I take a sip of water.

"Talking of Mum – which I'd rather not – I can't forgive her for what she did to you. I only found out recently. Well I won't be seeing her again. She was the start of most of my problems. I never knew why she wanted me to be a medic – me! I just wanted to make money, which I did once I'd dropped out, selling dope, easy money until I got caught."

I unzip my bag just to check the cash is there. Passport's in my pocket – Ellie thought I'd lost it, but it was just a ploy.

"It's Ellie I feel sorry for. I'd always fancied her even when she was still married to Danny. Anyway, Dad, I've written this letter to her. I hope you don't mind if I read it to you. I kept a copy.

Dear Ellie

I've never been any good at telling you personal stuff – face to face I mean.

It was all great when we started, an instant family – me, who couldn't have kids.

But we lost our way didn't we and I'm not really cut out to be a dad. And I couldn't handle all that stuff about your past.

No doubt Mum will be round, bothering you. My advice is to stay away from her – but you probably don't need me to tell you that.

Oh, and the same goes for Jim. You must realise he's had his eye on you – he's so bloody obvious. Steer clear of him. I mean he's a good drinking partner – he's the reason I've put so much weight on - but beyond that there's nothing there. And he still owes me money.

As for the business – I've had to wind it up. I've put some money in your account to tide you over.

That's about it really. As you've probably guessed, I won't be coming back.

Thanks for the good times.

Steven

"Do you think that sounds OK, Dad? I was never any good with words. Frankie said she'd post it for me, once I'm out of the country. You always had a soft spot for Frankie. Well I did ask her to come with me, but she turned me down. It was a bit of a shock. She said I shouldn't confuse liking with loving."

I notice the headstone is flaking, pick out a sliver and put it in my pocket, something I can hang on to when I think of Dad.

"I've kept it to myself, but the business did really well, although you won't be surprised to hear that I sailed too close to the wind. I can do with figures what I can't do with words and there are plenty of people who want their books sorted out – creatively - if I can put it that way. I got rid of the evidence, paperwork shredded, laptop wiped, hard drive destroyed. Bit of a job that.

"So this is it, Dad. I've got my usual train to catch and then a plane. Not sure where yet. I won't forget you, I promise."

ONE HUNDRED YEARS ON

Virginia Hainsworth

To those of you who could not go to war
but stayed at home to fight the fight
in factories and lonely homes,
condemned to wait, and mourn your sons,
your fathers, husbands, brothers too.
We applaud you.

To those of you who boldly went
and not so boldly, too, but still you went,
to rot alive in rat infested trench.
You fought the fear, withstood the pain,
returning home as strangers in a land forever changed.
We thank you.

To those of you who gave your all,
who sacrificed the precious life you had,
whose final days were terror filled,
brave enough to show your dread, yet braver still
to hide it, too, for others' sake.
We salute you.

To all of you who lived your days
one hundred years before our given time,
whose love, whose youth, whose limbs, whose lives
were spent in blood, whose skies were full of darkness,
whose hope extinguished lay, yet rose anew.
We owe you.

THE DAY MY HUSBAND LEFT FOR MARS

Clair Wright

The day my husband left for Mars, we had beans on toast for tea. We sat around the table, the children and I, stabbing beans with our forks, and looking out of the window at the dusky sky, wondering if one of the little silvery dots was him.

I cried, of course, when he told me.

"You might as well be dead," I said.

Tom said it wasn't like that. He said we would stay in touch, with video messages and emails.

He said, "Just think how proud the kids will be, when their dad is one of the first humans on Mars."

I said, "They won't have a dad anymore."

He said, "This is a once in a lifetime chance."

I said, "What about your life with us? What about our life together?"

He said, "This has always been my dream – to be an explorer, to be a hero."

I said, "I dreamed of growing old with you."

He said, "Please don't try to stop me."

Tom bought the new Lego Mars set for the children, and James spent hours constructing the model habitation pods and rover vehicles, moving the little astronauts in their Mars suits around the encampment.

"Look, maybe this one is Daddy!" he said, and I had to look away.

I didn't go to the launch. I stayed at home, and washed

the kitchen floor, tile by tile. James and Catherine went with Tom's sister. James took the little Lego astronaut with him, clutched tightly in his fist. I don't think they really understood that he wasn't coming back. How could they?

After he'd gone, I grieved. It was a strange sort of grief – angry, despairing, lonely, disbelieving - but interrupted with emails and messages from Tom, from 'the other side'. He wrote about space-sickness and dehydrated food. He said he missed us.

Mum and Dad brought round pies and hotpots to make sure we were all eating properly, and I pushed the food around my plate, trying to hide bits under my cutlery like a naughty child. Tom's parents came too, but I could hardly bear to look at their stricken faces, the mirror of my own.

My friends were divided. There were those in the "forget him!" camp who talked as if Tom had left me – I suppose he had. This camp urged me to get out, start having fun, start dating. Unthinkable – in my head I was still married - a Mars widow.

The other camp didn't know what to say to me. They averted their eyes, crossed the street to avoid an awkward meeting. I didn't blame them.

It's been a month since Tom left. He wanted to be a hero, but it turns out that the world soon gets bored of grainy pictures of people floating around a space-ship. He's old news now, until something more exciting happens - they blow up, they crash land, they kill each other – something like that. After all, it will be eight months until they even reach Mars.

I am, however, much more news-worthy. The week

after the launch, I was on TV. I sat on the daytime chat show sofa, opposite the sympathetic host with a tear in her eye.

"And how are you feeling now?" she asked, her head on one side, to emphasise her concern. "Do you worry about him?"

And it was then that I realised that I barely thought about Tom, hour by hour, day by day. I didn't wonder what he was doing, or worry whether he was safe. I was too busy dealing with his absence.

I didn't say any of this, of course. I smiled, bravely, and I said, "I am so proud of my husband. He is fulfilling his dream, and that is enough for me." The audience erupted into spontaneous applause. The Twitter feed went into overdrive. The show went into a feature on hair-care in zero gravity, but, at that moment, I became a worldwide icon for the brave, selfless wife.

Now our daily life is consumed greedily, examined and discussed, scrutinised and shared. We are followed, we are photographed; there is talk of a movie. Everyone knows who we are, and there is no escape, no possibility of return to our old lives.

Tom hurtles on in his claustrophobic capsule, into forever. He has left us, but by an equal and opposite reaction, we are leaving him, too.

At night, I dream of space. I am hanging, lightly tethered to a bit of rock, cocooned in a cumbersome suit and helmet. I am surrounded by a deep blackness, scattered with tiny points of light. I cannot touch anything. I reach out with my gloved hand and there is nothing, and more nothing. I am adrift.

GILBERT'S BIRTHDAY

A collaborative story told backwards by
Annabel Howarth, Inez Cook, Suzanne Hudson
& Emma Harding

80th

Knock, knock, knock. "Gilbert… Gilbert, it's Annie. Are you there?"

I am there - lying in bed, eyes tightly shut, hoping that Annie will give up and go away for a while. It's my birthday - one of those milestone ones, which someone always wants to mark, but not me. I need time to prepare, to face the day. I can sense Annie is still there. I picture her head leaning against the door, listening. So I stay still, holding my breath, my heart pounding in my head. She is whispering, probably to Molly. I can hear them shuffle away. I can breathe.

Today I am 80. I tried to hide it, but there's no hiding anything at The Elms Residential Home. I don't mind being 80. I just don't want the questions from others, and the memories creeping in, reminding me of my regrets. You can't hide from your memories though, and by letting anyone in, even a little, you can't avoid the questions either.

I am happy, here, at The Elms. We are lucky that most of us have our faculties about us, and I am enjoying a life I once thought impossible, for me. I've been here about 18 months. Recently I realised that the main source of my happiness is Annie. She is beautiful, funny, intelligent and we share a passion for music.

Annie arrived here about a week after me. She had recently lost her husband and didn't want to be alone. I told her I was in the same situation, having lost my wife Joanna. She assumed I meant Joanna had recently died too. I didn't correct her, so in some ways, you could say our friendship was built on a lie. It didn't feel that way to me though. I felt I was mourning the loss of Joanna, as though it had just happened, and it was easier to let the belief form that, that was how I ended up here, rather than have to explain where I'd been for the past 27 years.

When Annie realised it was going to be my 80th birthday, she wouldn't let go of the fact my family wouldn't be coming to see me. She never had children of her own, but her nephews and nieces all dote on her. She is often going somewhere for a weekend with one or other of them or their children, whereas I have nowhere else to go.

Yesterday Annie quizzed me again as she studied the photos on my desk. The one in the dark wooden frame is my favourite photo of my mother, as I remember her from childhood, before it all went wrong. The photo in the ornate silver frame is of Joanna, me and my step-son, Peter, on our wedding day. We all look so happy then. The other framed photo is my favourite one of my daughter Lizzie, aged about 6, twirling round, her skirt flying and she smiling with her big indigo eyes looking straight at the camera. A small unframed photo leans against it. It is of Lizzie on her wedding day, with her husband whose name I don't even know. It's an action shot I took with a polaroid camera. She is coming towards the back of the church, staring past me. Did she even know I was there? I do feel a certain amount of guilt about that. She didn't invite me, and asked her mother to tell me not to come, but I did anyway. I came in and stood at the back of the church, feeling entitled to be at my own daughter's wedding, but looking back, I wonder now if I had that right.

Annie sees the best in me, and can't understand why I'm here all alone, knowing that I have a daughter, a step-son, and possibly grandchildren I know nothing about.

I say, "You don't know the things I've done."

She laughs and says, "What could you possibly have done that's so bad, Gilbert. You are the most gentlemanly man I've ever known."

I smile back and say, "My demons are tired now, Annie. Can we leave them alone?"

She says, "OK. Let's leave the past in the past."

But I fear that today she will look at me with those pitying eyes and I can't face them.

Knock, knock, knock. It's Annie again.

"Gilbert?"

"Just a minute, Annie." I put on my dressing gown and slippers and unlock the door.

"Happy Birthday, Gilbert," she beams. She hands me a bottle of my favourite single malt with a bow on it, and a wrapped gift that could be a book, no doubt a spy novel, as she knows I like them. She doesn't look pitying. She looks excited. "I have a day full of surprises in store for you," she says.

I smile and kiss her on her cheek. She blushes. I feel a glow in my tummy and think, "This day is not going to be so bad after all."

51st

Lizzie and her husband step out of the church and I just manage to hide from view by crouching behind a hedge. She looks just like her mum did on our wedding day. She giggles as friends and family throw confetti and her husband leads her by the hand to their car. He brushes some stray confetti out of her hair and I sense that she hasn't done badly at all. Before I can suppress it, a smile creeps onto my face. Their car moves off and my hand grips the Polaroid in my pocket. At least I got one photo – one memory to keep. That's more than I deserve.

Family and friends make their way out of the churchyard. Joanna turns around and I can't tell whether she's looking at me or the church doors. I remain still and try to read her expression but she turns again and hurries to join the others. She was never one to linger. Once her mind was set about the car accident, she made sure I lost everything and everyone. Who could blame her, the way I behaved in the aftermath? My thoughts are broken by a sharp tap on my shoulder.

"Peter!" I hug my stepson and carry on holding him, remembering the little boy who used to run into my arms.

"I saw you coming into the church. Late as usual," he jokes, fully aware I wasn't allowed to come. I splutter and laugh. I haven't seen his face for so long.

"How is your mum? Does Lizzie know I'm here?" It all tumbles out of me at once.

"No. Mum says today is the happiest day we've had for a long time. Best keep it that way."

I nod. "Who gave Lizzie away?"

"Me. She asked me to. Want some? It's your favourite." He grins, pulling out a hip flask, knowing I'll be tempted. "Dutch courage. She asked me to do the father of the bride speech too."

I search his eyes as he takes a swig but I know where I stand. The warmth has left his voice. I try to change the subject.

"Do you remember what you and I were doing exactly this time last year?"

"Yep. Watching the latest Bond film. For your 50th." He pauses to look me in the eye. "And two weeks after that you smashed us both into a tree. Remember that? How dare you show up today. Did you want to explain yourself? Be forgiven and everything go back to normal?"

"I was hoping nobody would see me today," I lie. In reality I held out an impossible hope that my family would still feel some love for me. Peter shakes his head in disgust.

"As always, you turn up when you're not wanted, and when someone needs you, you're nowhere to be seen. If you can't be the hero, you run away. This isn't one of your stupid spy novels. It was my life. When I needed you most, you ran away."

I see tears in his eyes and think back to the last time I saw his face. It was bloodied and bruised. He was slumped out cold in the passenger seat. I stumbled out of the driver's seat and into the night, gripping my car keys in one hand and my bottle in another. It was easy to hide in the dark as I watched the paramedics take him away. I tossed the bottle into some bushes and ran. I was scared of being caught. Even more terrifying, however, was the thought of having to face any of those authorities again.

I've been running ever since.

"You know, Peter, meeting you and your mum was the best thing to ever happen to me." In those heady days of new love I believed I could lay the past to rest and make something good in my life last. I did, for a while. "When I hit that tree, the old me resurfaced. The same old fears, the same old messing things up. It was all I could manage to run."

He looks at me in silence and I see in his face that there is no love, just pity. He turns and walks away, pausing to shout back, "Happy birthday, Gil."

My fist clenches. I swallow back my anger and thrust my hand into my pocket, clasping my passport and flight tickets. Through the hedge, I watch my stepson for the last time as he leaves the churchyard and approaches his car. He takes his time getting into the driver's seat, lifting in his left leg and then using his hands to lift in his right leg. I see that where his right ankle and foot should be, there is a prosthesis covered by his sock and polished shoe.

30th

You hope that after seven years inside, people might forget, but not around here. I was barely out when the taunting started. People staring in the street, fingers pointing, whispers and jeers. Mothers holding their children to them, as I passed, as though I might harm them just by looking at them. Shopkeepers ignoring me, until I stopped going in and had to drive two miles just to get bread and milk.

The people at AA understood. Barry had been through it and Dervla. They said keep your head down, keep sober, time is a great healer and people will see that you've changed. Bernie has always served me at the chip shop though. I don't usually go in on a Friday night, but it's my 30th birthday today and even though no one knows or cares, I want to mark the occasion somehow. Just as Bernie is about to take my order, the local kingpin Jez and three of his cronies stumble in, beer cans in their hands, push me to one side and begin shouting their orders at Bernie. His chubby face breaks into a grin, but he's no pushover.

"Hang on a minute lads," he says amicably. "I think Gilbert here was next."

Jez turns to look at me with pure hate. "That scumbag?"

"Come on now, Jezzie boy. Look, let me just get Gilbert served and then we'll sort you boys out with some fodder." A queue is now beginning to form behind me and the people in it watch the goings on with unease.

Please, I think. Please just let him get me my food so I can get out of here.

"So you'd rather serve a drink driving child murderer than me and my buddies?" Jez shouts, grabbing Bernie's neck across the counter, so that the blubbery skin under Bernie's chin balloons out over his shirt collar, like a huge blister about to burst. I deserve it, but not Bernie, the only guy around here who tolerates me.

I launch myself at Jez and as he lets go of Bernie, his punch hits me hard on my right cheek and I feel myself crashing into some of the customers at tables, sending their fish and chips flying. No one comes to my rescue. There is a shocked silence, then a muted cheer and some cackling from the young girls in the queue. Jez's mates hold him back as I pick myself up off the floor and stumble out of

The Fat Frier.

I slope home like a wounded dog, reeking of vinegar, keeping to the shadows. I wish Jez and his pals had dragged me outside and finished off the job properly, dumping my body around the back of the shops with the bins.

Triple locked inside my shabby little flat, I begin to make a plan.

***

I drive for an hour to reach the forest. I want to be far away from all of them. I don't want any of them to find me. They would love it. They would still be mocking me, even in death. The thick rope sits curled in the Spar carrier bag on the passenger seat, a magic serpent that will take me away from all of this forever.

I pull up at an isolated parking area with two empty cars. Dog walkers no doubt, gone for hours. As I lock up and walk into the thick forest I catch myself mentally getting my bearings so that I can find my way back to the car, and then realise with a jolt that there is no need, because I won't be coming back.

I tried to make a fresh start, got a job in a warehouse in Sackville Road on the outskirts of town, where the mainly Pakistani workforce didn't know my history. Eight years sober, I kept myself to myself, taking one day at a time, like they'd told me at AA. Those guys at the weekly meetings had saved me. Without them I would have been back on the drink, probably back in prison. But I still see her face all the time, her smile turning to a look of horror just before I hit her. And I still see her little body bouncing off my bonnet. She will never leave me and I can't stand it a minute longer.

As I follow a path through the forest I hear voices nearby. There is a turn in the path and up ahead I can see a clearing, with some wooden climbing equipment. A young boy, about two or three years old, is kicking a football to his mother, who keeps missing it and has to run to retrieve it.

I keep my head down, trying to act normally, like a guy out for a stroll. As I walk through the play area the little boy runs up, holding his ball out towards me. I freeze. His mother comes over, trying to grab his hand.

"Peter!" she laughs, and then turns to me. "I'm sorry, I hope he's not pestering you. It's just he misses kicking a ball around, since his dad…"

"It's fine," I find myself saying, recognising the pain behind her eyes and realising this stranger is the first person who has looked at me without hate or pity for as long as I can remember.

The boy puts down his ball and kicks it to me. The ball lies at my feet and the boy looks up at me, expectantly waiting. The woman looks at me too, smiling in gratitude already. For a moment, I see myself in their eyes, a kind stranger, willing to make a little lad happy. I put down my carrier bag and I kick the ball back to the boy.

10th

"You look really pretty, Mummy."

Mummy gives me a big squeeze. "Well, thank you, darling," she says. "I wanted to look nice for your birthday." She leans back and smiles at me. "How does it feel to be ten?"

I think about this for a bit. To be honest I don't really feel any different to how I felt yesterday but I know that I am, somehow. "I feel very grown-up, I think."

Mummy laughs. "My little man," she says. "It's good to know I have you to look after me."

"Just while Daddy's away," I say. She stops laughing and looks at me for a long time.

"Yes, dear," she says after a bit. "Just while Daddy's away."

"Tell me what he's doing again."

"Oh Gilly, I've told you so many times." She turns away from me.

"But Mummy, it's my birthday and I want to hear about Daddy."

Without looking at me, she says, "OK then, just this one time and no more OK?"

"OK," I say, bringing my knees up under my chin. I love this story. Mummy starts, as always, by telling me about how Daddy went off to fight in the war when I was four. I don't remember much about him apart from his shiny black shoes and how he smelt of barley sugar. Because Daddy was so brave, Mummy says, he was recruited by the British Government to be a spy. Right now, he's on a secret mission far away. No one except the Prime Minister knows where he is. One day though he'll come home and everything will be different.

"Different how, Mummy?" I ask, as I always do.

She sighs. "We'll live in a big house with an outhouse that doesn't leak when it rains. I'll have a different dress for every day of the week and you'll have new shoes. We'll have a roast chicken every Sunday and fresh eggs every morning…"

"What's roast chicken like, Mummy?" I say, but she's still talking, her voice getting louder and faster.

"… We'll live somewhere where the neighbours aren't all nosey buggers with nothing better to do than gossip. Somewhere where we'll get a bit of respect. Somewhere decent. Somewhere where I wouldn't have to…" She stops.

"Where you wouldn't have to what, Mummy?" She looks at me as if she'd forgotten I was there.

"Nothing, darling. Come on now, or you'll be late for school."

"Awww." I say. I hate school. "Why do I have to go to school on my birthday? It's not fair."

Mummy looks tired. "You're right Gilly, it's not fair. Nothing in this life is fair. The sooner you learn that the better off you'll be. Now get yourself to school."

***

Loud voices are coming from the kitchen when I come home. Perhaps it's a party for me. I push open the kitchen door, excitement rising inside me like bubbles in a bottle of pop, but it's only Mummy and Uncle Bob. I'd forgotten it was a Wednesday. Uncle Bob's always here on a Wednesday.

"Alright there, Gilly lad?" he says, ruffling my hair with his big rough hands. Mummy watches us, frowning. She's wearing her housecoat now and her hair is down. She doesn't look as pretty as she did this morning.

"It's my birthday today," I tell him.

"Is it now?" he says. "Well ain't that somethin'? Happy

birthday lad." He looks at Mummy.

"You'd better go now, Bob," she says and turns away, reaching up to put the money tin on the highest shelf in the cupboard. From there, she takes out a bottle of yellowish-brown liquid and pours some into a glass.

"Whatever you say, Aud," Uncle Bob says, letting himself out of the back door. "You're the boss. See you next week, Gilly." As he crosses the yard he waves his hand at me, then pulls his cap hard onto his head, pulls his shoulders up and disappears through the gate.

"Can I have some?" I ask, pointing at Mummy's drink.

She laughs. "No dear, it's just for grown-ups. You wouldn't like the taste." She looks at her glass, swirling the liquid around. "Besides, it's too precious to waste - you have no idea what I had to do to get this."

She sounds sad. She's about to say more but then there's a tap-ta-ta-tap on the door and Mrs Williams from down the road steps into the kitchen.

"Happy birthday, Gilly," she says smiling like the cat in the Alice in Wonderland story. She hands me a small brown paper parcel, "Something for your collection." She picks up the kettle. "How about a nice cup of tea, Audrey?" she says.

Mummy drops into a chair as if she was a ragdoll. Mrs Williams looks at me. "Why don't you go and play in the other room, dear?" she says.

I take my present into the front parlour. I hope it's what I think it is. Yes! A racing car. Brilliant! In good condition too. I settle down on the rug - let's see how fast you can go.

Then I hear Mummy shouting. "No! I can't tell him, Vy, he'd hate me. It'd screw him up for life." Then she says, "I know, I know. But I've been lying for so long - how can I tell him now?" Then she yells even louder. "You interfering old bat! How dare you? What dirty minds you and all your cronies have. Like I'd ever do anything so, so demeaning!" There's the sound of the door slamming shut and then it all goes quiet. I go into the kitchen. Mummy's at the kitchen table, her head on her arms.

"Mummy?" I say.

"Go away, Gilly," she says, her voice muffled.

"But, Mummy."

"Now, Gilly!"

Why is she shouting at me? I run from the room and pound up the stairs to my bedroom. Bloody Mummy. She's always cross. I try to be good but she gets mad anyway.

Later, she comes into my room with a glass of warm milk and some toast and dripping on a tray. She's all dressed up again. "I'm sorry, Gilly," she says. "I'm just worn out." She's got another glass of that golden drink. She kneels beside me. "What a rotten birthday you've had," she says, brushing my hair out of my eyes. "Why don't you put your pyjamas on, get into bed and I'll read you a story?"

As I change, she picks up my milk and tips some of her drink into mine. "A grown-up drink for a grown-up little man," she says, handing it to me.

I take a sip. It tastes mostly of milk but there's something else which catches on the back of my throat and makes me cough. It's nice.

"Tomorrow," she says quietly as I snuggle into bed, "I'm going to tell you the truth about something. Something I should have told you a long time ago."

"OK, Mummy," I say, sleepily. There's a warm glow in my tummy. Nothing can hurt me. Mummy and I will look after each other and Daddy will be home soon.

UP A MOUNTAIN IN KOSOVO

Inez Cook

On a clear and cold April morning, we leave the town of Ferizaj where we are staying and head south towards the mountains. We come off the highway and onto a dusty road, then pull in at a mini-supermarket. We are here to pick up Hysen, the mountain man who is going to take us up Lybeten, one of the tallest and most beautiful peaks in Kosovo. Outside the tired-looking building, with its faded cigarette and soft drinks posters, three children sit playing on the ground. This is the only store for miles which provides essentials for local villagers. Hysen's family has owned it for two decades. The room beside the shop is a café and in the hot summer the plastic white furniture comes out, whilst in the harsh winter the chessboards come out.

Hysen appears at the shop door and we climb out of the dusty car to greet him. He is a sturdy man in his late 50s, with a mountain-weathered face and a smile of rugged serenity. When I shake his hand, it feels rough from many years of manual work. He is going to take us up to his house near the top of the mountain, where in the warmer months he takes his herd of sheep and goats and spends time in solitude. He apologises for not speaking English and occasionally shifts from his native Albanian into German. Limited job prospects here mean that many families have a breadwinner living in western Europe. German is, therefore, the second language for many

Kosovans with links to the diaspora communities in Switzerland, Germany and Austria.

After the customary greetings, we set off in our car, with Hysen leading the way in his car. We begin up the winding hairpin road at the foot of the mountain, forest on both sides, until we reach the point where we change vehicle and go off-road. Hysen is already waiting for us, his hand gently resting on our mountain vehicle. It is a dull green Lada Niva from the 1970s, Russia's answer to the Landrover, and a reminder of Kosovo's communist past as part of Yugoslavia. From the outside it looks more like an army relic than a usable vehicle, but under the bonnet it is well-maintained. Vehicles are a big investment for many poor families, so they are extremely well looked after and older models are often reconditioned to last a long time. As he holds out his hand to help each of us into its high cabin, Hysen jokes that it is the only vehicle that can manage the higher mountain tracks.

Shortly after we set off, we see a man descending the track on a horse and cart. He passes us with his eyes lowered. The cart is full of logs and Hysen explains he is an illegal logger. Most Kosovan houses are heated with woodburners and so the logs are an essential resource. Hysen affectionately calls him Robin Hood. For the first part of the journey, there is still forest on either side of the rocky road and at times, with our centre of gravity much higher, it feels as if we are almost vertical. It is a deciduous forest and the trees that we pass are familiar: oak, birch and beech. It takes a bumpy half hour to reach the higher part of the mountain which opens onto lush green pasture, and then a further ten minutes to reach Hysen's mountain house. Next to the house, the track continues upwards until the grass recedes to a white carpet of snow which stretches as far as the mountain peak. Out of the earthy shade of the forest, the quality of light here is very different. The green fields are bright and lush and the sun on the snow is almost blinding. Even at our destination it is still a three-hour trek to the peak. We climb out of the Niva and walk towards Hysen's house as he explains that the last of the snow will not melt until late summer.

We are glad to get out of the cold when we step inside the house. The room we enter has rough white plastered walls and is empty apart from a single mattress, plastic chairs and a woodburning stove in the middle of the room. Hysen invites us to sit as he hangs his shotgun on a hook behind the door. He explains he must keep it to hand at all times, as the wild animals on the mountain include bears and wolves.

After collecting firewood from the store outside, he deftly lays and lights the stove. The warmth spreads and shortly after the teapot is whistling on the stove. Hysen is preparing Turkish tea, a remnant of the Ottoman Empire in the history of Kosovo. It is also a central tradition in Kosovo-Albanian hospitality, where guests are afforded great respect and are regarded with an almost regal courtesy. He uses a blue enamel double teapot. The pot on top is made into a strong tea and then diluted using the water from the lower pot. It is taken black with sugar and is served in a small curved glass. Hysen opens a carrier bag and lays out some tomatoes and a generous bunch of wild garlic leaves. He gestures to us to help ourselves, reminding me of the Albanian saying which sums up the simple tenets of hospitality here: *buk, krip e zemer* (bread, salt and heart).

A little later we are joined by brothers Bajrush and Bekim, friends of Hysen and our hosts during our stay. They are windswept and tired as they step into the house, grateful to be at the end of their two-hour trek up the mountain. After our tea, Hysen sets up his chessboard and challenges Bekim to play. They settle down on the mattress and, in the quiet concentration of the game, I realise how loud the wind and vehicle clatter were on our way up. The room is silent until Hysen, acknowledging defeat, knocks over Bekim's King. The pieces scatter and laughter fills the room.

Hysen shows us the three unfinished rooms of the house. The largest room contains wooden animal enclosures lined with straw, ready for Hysen's goat herd that will come and graze in the summer. The second room will eventually be used to store homemade cheese and pickles. The third room contains metal bunk beds and blankets for travellers to use. It will be used on 1st August, Hysen explains, when hundreds of people from surrounding villages climb Lybeten and camp overnight. By then the snow has melted and walkers can see the glacial lake that sits just behind the summit. Hysen describes how Lybeten holds a sacred significance for locals and how national identity is closely connected to the landscape. Kosovo lies on a plain surrounded by mountains. This means that wherever you are in the country, the mountains always remain in sight. For centuries, as well as providing sustenance to people, the mountains have been revered for being a natural fortress against invaders.

Hysen points out a small stream a few yards away from the house. A concrete trough siphons off some of the stream water down to a small water-wheel. The wheel has been hand-cut and hammered from tin and is connected to a generator which will eventually provide the house with electricity. The house and its handmade hydro-power system have taken years to build, as all the building materials have had to be transported by car. The project is a long-term one, and despite his ingenuity and resilience, Hysen is aware that it always remains subject to his health and the mountain weather conditions.

We walk to a grass ridge as Bajrush and Bekim gather kindling. Every so often Hysen looks up and scans the mountainside. He tells us that there are certain places where it is best not to walk. Since the war in 1999, most unexploded mines have been cleared by NATO but he is still cautious. We huddle around the newly-lit fire. The flames seem strangely intimate next to the vast drop a few feet behind us. Warming his hands, Hysen tells us about his mother. He says the mountain kept her healthy and the clean air and mineral-rich springs were the secrets to her longevity. He smiles as he speaks and I see how he has transformed during the journey. Far from his shop where he first greeted us with stoic reserve, up here he is in his element, the guarded alertness occasionally thawing to reveal a man at ease and at home in this landscape.

Around where we are sitting, the grass is dotted purple and yellow. Hysen points and names each one: wild violets and celandine. These tiny bright flowers seem incongruous with the bare branches of the woods below but even on a wintry April day the richness of the biodiversity is clear. This region is particularly known for its butterflies, including some very rare and endangered species. Apart from the illegal logging it is unspoilt, making it an area of interest for conservation research.

A little later, Bekim spots an eagle dipping below us. We walk closer to the ridge to follow its descent. Through a thin layer of cloud the city of Ferizaj is visible and beyond that the capital Prishtina. Up here it is almost possible to forget that there was a war in recent past. After collecting our things, we climb back into Hysen's Lada and start our descent. Hysen points out a helicopter circling a neighbouring mountain. It belongs to KFOR, the NATO organisation in charge of peace-keeping. Soon other signs of war start to reappear, the shells of burned-out houses and empty villages. Our journey off the mountain takes us along the same route that the villagers took in 1999 to flee violence. In two days we will attend a memorial service to commemorate the local civilians killed during the conflict. For now though, we clatter down the mountain and say goodbye to Hysen, grateful that he invited us to share the thing most precious to him: his mountain.

IT'S THE LOVE THAT LASTS

Annabel Howarth

What was more shocking - the fact that my 50 year old second cousin had died, or that I found out on Facebook? Or was it the fact that I cried? I cried like I loved him, really loved him, yet I hadn't seen him in at least three years, and following that occasion I'd decided I really wouldn't mind if I never saw him again.

He barely acknowledged me, and I was appalled at the person he'd become. It was at my brother's house. I'd travelled a long way to see my brother, and Terry was there. He'd become a frequent visitor. He was a mess, and was looking to my brother for support, but it was too much for him. It wasn't the fact that Terry needed help which bothered me though. It was the fact that he seemed so utterly self centred, that his needs and his suffering were so much more important than the needs of anyone else; that he seemed so oblivious to others. I had an hour to spend with my brother, and he'd told Terry he couldn't see him when he called, but he turned up anyway. He'd met a girl, and he had to tell my brother all about it there and then. Needless to say, I didn't get to speak to my brother that day.

In the six months or so that my brother and Terry were close, my brother had rescued Terry after a suicide attempt at least twice. He tried to help him face up to his problems, but he was in denial. My brother had problems of his own, so was sympathetic and wanted to help, but he wasn't equipped to do so.

But when I cried, I wasn't only crying for his family: his long-suffering parents, his sister, his children and his grandchildren left behind, or my brother who I knew would carry some guilt that he couldn't help him. When I was crying, my head was filled with memories. Memories of when we were younger. Memories from before it all seemed to go wrong. There were 10 years between us, and he had been the cool older cousin admired from afar. He was handsome, friendly and funny. He reminded me of my first childhood crush, a young John Travolta. When I was a teenager, he would sometimes give me a lift home from school if he was passing. As a self-conscious fifteen year old, I went for a ride on the back of his motorbike - the first and last ever time - it was exhilarating and I loved every second of it. I can still picture the moment, with my arms wrapped around his leather jacket as we leant into the corners; feel and hear the crunch of the leather, the roar of the engine, the wind catching the ends of my long hair and the heaviness of the helmet; and that feeling that I wanted the moment to last forever. And it has. And it will. Another treasured memory was an evening in my early twenties, when we shared a few drinks and the family secrets - slightly embellished, but very amusing.

Interestingly, the day before I heard the news, I was having lunch with friends, when one of the ladies said how moved she'd been by the media reports following the brutal stabbing of Ann Maguire by one of her pupils. Ann was reported to have been such a loving person who did so much for so many people, and there was a huge outpouring of love for her. One of the men in our group said that, though he didn't know Ann and had no reason to think anything that was said about her wasn't true, it always surprised him how people are exalted when they die and held up to be saints. He used the example of his own headmaster's funeral, where he was said to be the saviour of his school, when he was anything but. We are none of us so perfect as we might appear to be at our funerals.

Isn't that the way it should be? There are some lost souls we might think devoid of love and conscience, take Jimmy Saville as an example; but for the rest of us, we are perfectly imperfect in our own way. We all have a darker side and have done things we are less proud of, but in the end, it's the love that lasts, as love never dies, and that is how we should and will be remembered. So hopefully, I will be able to go to my second cousin's funeral, and if I do, although the last moments we shared together were not the best, I will be there with the rest of them, celebrating and remembering the love in his life, and the loving ways in which he touched mine.

DISCOVERING BERLIN

Clair Wright

There were a few raised eyebrows when we told people that our first trip abroad with our children was to be to Berlin. We were to visit my cousin Lucy who lives in the city. It was to be an adventure, and we hoped William (7), and Oliver (5), would think so too.

Berlin seems to be a city struggling with its history; it is raw and present. Along the street, running through the buses and cyclists and 'Trabant Safaris', is a line of cobbles –the route of the Berlin Wall. It runs like a scar through the centre of the city. The boys enjoy spotting the line as we follow our guidebook between the city's landmarks.

"Are we in the East, or the West, now?" William asks.

It's hard to tell, and I try to imagine the ugly concrete barrier towering above us. Here and there are tall posts showing its height and thickness. At the Eastside Gallery, a stretch of the wall has been preserved, painted with murals depicting images of reconciliation and peace. Signs forbid its defacement, but graffiti and fly-posts are defiantly evident, as if declaring, *it's our wall now*.

We visit the Holocaust Memorial. Austere grey blocks of different sizes are arranged in a grid. The ground undulates disconcertingly under our feet, so that as we enter, we begin to descend and the blocks tower above us on each side. William and Oliver are excited, running between the blocks as though in a maze. We call anxiously after them as they disappear from sight. We catch fleeting glimpses of other people as they pass between the blocks around us then disappear.

I call the boys to us and try to explain the memorial.

"It is to remember millions of people who died, in the war," I say.

"Were killed," Lucy corrects, and I know she is right. We shouldn't soften the truth with gentler words. The boys nod solemnly, and then run off again. Of course they can't understand. Neither can we.

In the Museum of Technology the boys clamber over full size fishing boats, pointing at planes hanging precariously above us. As they explore the engine sheds, we read the exhibits. A display tells of the transportation of the Jews, and the collaboration of the railways with the Nazis. An interactive screen allows visitors to access records of trains leaving each town, and their passengers. Even here, there is no escape from history's shadow.

The restored Reichstag building, proud with its giant German flag, has a glass cupola, open to the sky. Glass, it seems, is a popular choice for Germany's restoration. We climb the ramp that spirals around the cupola, enjoying the views over the city, listening to our audio guide, available in many languages. Berlin welcomes the world into its glass, transparent heart.

As we travel home we discuss the best bits of our trip.

Oliver chooses trams. William chooses trains. I choose discovering in our own way, together.

RIPPLES

Emma Harding

It's not a good day for sailing. There's barely a breath of wind and the sea is lake-smooth. But it's the first time we've had a weekend free in an absolute age so we're determined to make the best of it. The boat rocks slightly as we clamber aboard, as if in resentful greeting. It's been over a year since we've done any decent sailing.

Onboard, we quickly fall into a familiar rhythm. Bill is up on deck optimistically unfurling the mainsail from its cover, gathering ropes from the storage boxes under the seats and checking fuel and battery levels. Me, I'm in the cabin stowing away provisions for our trip, locating charts and the logbook and switching on the radio. The air is stale down here and the bunk cushions smell musty. There is a sheen of salt-sticky dust over everything and I resolve to spend at least some of the trip down here giving the place a bit of a spruce. While Bill prepares the sheets and the sail for hoisting I take the opportunity to put on my sailing gear. I have learnt from experience to dress for all weathers. However warm and sunny it might appear onshore, it can still be bitingly cold out at sea. I scrape my hair back and tuck it under an old baseball cap. It's not an attractive look, I'll grant you, but wind, salt-spray and hair are not a happy mix. Luckily, there are no mirrors onboard.

Preparations complete, we set about the process of departing. Again we perform our allotted tasks wordlessly, a well-rehearsed, syncopated dance, each of our manoeuvres in time with the other's. I'm on the pontoon, having loosened both the bow and stern mooring lines but still holding onto both. Bill starts the engine which coughs into life, disgorging a spurt of water out behind. I push the bow hard away from me and leap onto the boat giving a final push against the pontoon edge as I do so. While Bill steers us gently out of the marina I pull the protective fenders up from the side of the boat and put them away. A pair of swans glides silently past us, pursued by their fluffy offspring and trailing ripples behind them.

The boat chugs its way out of the marina and into open sea. There's still no wind to speak of and no point hoisting the sails. There's nothing for me to do. The stench of diesel and the noise of the engine hangs heavy in the air. I look back at Bill from my position near the bow. His mouth is a tight line. He's so determined to be out on the water but I know he's frustrated. I turn my gaze forward again and shift my position so that I can lean my back against the empty mast. I'm supposed to be keeping a look out but there's nothing else out here so I close my eyes. Sailing's much more Bill's thing than mine. I get seasick when it's rough and I hate having to use marina facilities. But Bill's had this dream since he was a teenager. He bought this boat with the hard-earned savings from many an unfulfilling job. He deserves this. But my heart's not in it. I'd much rather be at home, if I'm honest, with a good book, or in my garden and within easy reach of a hot bath. And a proper toilet.

We're really very different, Bill and I. He's outdoorsy, likes camping and hiking. I like home comforts and convenience, good food and a warm bed. We've been married for over twenty years though despite our differences. And, I'll admit, we've had some real adventures on this boat. When the wind is up and waves are tipped with white, when the sails are taut and the boat leans and skims over the water as if greased. When your arms ache from winching and your eyes sting from seawater, voices hoarse from shouting at each other over the roar of the wind and the sea. That's when I saw what Bill loves about all this. How exhilarating it can be, how it can make you feel alive. And that's when I loved him the most, his skin tanned and glistening, his muscles taut with effort, his eyes bright with joy.

But that feels like a lifetime ago. When we were both young enough to throw ourselves into it. When it was all new to us. Today I feel ancient. Bulky, dumpy and sweaty in all this clobber. I feel becalmed. Going nowhere fast.

A gull shrieks overhead and I open my eyes. The glare of the sun bouncing off the varnished waters makes me squint. Time for a cup of tea, I think. I heave myself up and make my way along the deck to the stern. Bill hasn't changed position. Still standing stiffly upright with one hand on the tiller and the other on the railing, he stares grimly ahead. His skin is greyer now, like his thinning hair, and he has a portly look about him I hadn't noticed before. He doesn't look at me. I don't think he's any happier than I am.

I climb down into the cabin and set the kettle on the cantilevered stovetop. As it starts to boil, emitting a shrill whistle, I run a damp cloth over the wooden shelf that holds the mugs. The sticky residue doesn't budge. It's going to take more than that to clean it. I make the tea, carry the two mugs up on deck and hand one to Bill. I sit in the cockpit and we both silently sip.

I look out to sea once more. The light has become hazier and it's difficult to make out the horizon. The boat continues to slip through the inert water causing barely a ripple in its surface. If only there were some wind.

LEVEL FOUR

A collaborative walk on the wild side by
Andrew Shephard, Suzanne Hudson,
Annabel Howarth, Clair Wright,
Virginia Hainsworth & Dave Rigby

MICHAEL

After breakfast on the third day, we gather around the metal tables and chairs outside of the hotel. Seven middle-aged walkers, one fit leader, and me. No one is sitting down. The chairs are spotted with raindrops from an early shower. My shorts and tee-shirt are still damp from yesterday's twelve wet miles, but it's my feet and shoes that bother me more. Natasha, our leader, makes the route sound interesting. She warns of lung-busting ascents, sharp rocks, and sections where there is no clear path. She tells us we will cope with the extra distance; we are a good group. Good in what way exactly?

"It's a harder walk today, Level Four. Make sure you have plenty of water. It will get hot. I mean hot. There will be no willages until the end. We won't see single person, unless hunting or collecting honey. The locals don't walk unless car is broken."

"Hunting? Not with guns?" One of the vegetarians, Diana I think.

"Shotguns, yes."

"How horrible. What do they kill?"

"Anything. Wild boar, snakes, small birds. They can shoot whatever they like, it's private land. But don't worry;

they don't mind you walking through the estate. Everyone very friendly. But don't run away if you hear gunshots. He might think you're a deer." Everyone laughs. But you could mistake Diana for a deer. If she's a deer, what animal are the others? I will decide while I walk. I have found walking all day gives me ideas for my game.

I haven't asked Natasha where she's from. Greece, Romania? Somewhere with hills but no jobs, obviously. She's Lycra fit and a good listener, too, but tells us nothing about herself. Everyone wants their turn talking to teacher while we walk. There's one couple who spend more time talking to Natasha than they do to each other.

Jemma and Clive. The couple. I know their names because they're in the room next to mine. Nightmare, literally. They're polite to each other during the day but three glasses into the free wine at dinner they start arguing. Their rows wake me up. I hear them swearing, fighting, crying. Some holiday they're having.

I ask our leader and carrier of the first-aid kit to take a look at my blisters. I wipe a seat dry with my hand and take off my trainers. She squats down and stares at my toes. She raises one foot to look at the sole. She shakes her head, swishing her mane over my feet.

"Oh, my poor boy. Bad. You should read the brochure. It says everywhere, Level Four, experienced only. Boots. Trainers not good." Who reads brochures? I booked online, a last minute thing. I was in danger of disappearing into cyberspace and had to step back into a real world. It was sunny and flat on the tour company website. Natasha says I should spend the day in the village and take care of my blisters when the pharmacy opens at ten or eleven.

No way! I don't give in that easily. I know about Level Four. The game I'm working on goes up to Seven. The coding gets well complex after level three. I've shown the game to the others on my phone, but they're not interested, only Natasha. She got it right away.

The rain stops and the sun comes out. It's hot, like Natasha said. It's steep, like Natasha said. Every step for the first two hours is agony, but then I'm past feeling pain. We have lunch on a ridge blasted by a hot wind. We start to descend, winding slowly through a wood. Diana catches up with Natasha and me. She's red in the face and breathing heavily.

"How much further is it?"

"Depends how fast you walk. One hour, two probably."

"Did you see the sign, Natasha? The one in the tree. It doesn't mean hunting, does it?"

"Show me."

We walk back fifty yards where the rest of the group are in a circle debating the sign. Natasha puts down her rucksack and announces a drinks break. She rummages through her bag and pulls out her walking notes. I point my camera at the sign. It doesn't translate. I try Wikipedia, but there's no wi-fi, 3G, or phone signal. Natasha finds the place in the notes and starts to laugh.

"Oh yes, bees. We must divert to avoid the hives. We can rejoin the path further down." Natasha points a teacher's finger counting the group.

"Why only seven?" We look at each other to compute the missing walker.

Even Jemma hasn't noticed, but then she does. "Has anyone seen Clive?"

CHARLIE

"He was here a second ago…where's he gone?" Julie seems mildly irritated and gulps from her water bottle.

"Was he?" asks Jemma. "I was talking to Seamus, I thought he was behind us." We look up and down the path but there's no sign of Clive.

"Are you sure that he was here a second ago?" I challenge Julie. I can't stand vagueness.

"Well I thought he was, but I was walking with Pam."

"So you can't be sure?"

"Well no…"

"Oh for goodness sake, who was the last person to see Clive?" I ask. God, these people irritate me. They speak slowly, they think slowly. No wonder none of them have achieved anything in their lives. Everyone looks at each other blankly. A mild look of panic crosses Jemma's face. She reaches for her phone but can't get a signal. We all check ours again but to no avail.

"Someone must have seen him leave the path… he can't have just vanished." She tries to keep her voice steady, but I can tell she's concerned. Blank faces again. Natasha looks puzzled, but stays perfectly calm.

"Has he gone off to do a… you know?" she asks Jemma.

"A what?" Jemma replies, her voice rising now.

"A pee pee?"

Michael, the games designer, snorts with laughter. He sets me off. I have to stuff the collar of my polo top into my mouth.

"Well if he has, he's been a long time," chuckles Seamus. "Unless it was more than a pee pee!"

That sets us off again. Natasha doesn't laugh. Her pretty face has hardened. Jemma grabs Natasha's arm.

"What about the hunters? Could he be in danger?"

"He should be okay, but we need to find him quickly," Natasha says, pulling her rucksack on. The rest of us start to do the same.

"No, no... you must stay here," she says.

"You're not serious?" exclaims Diana.

"Yes, that is the correct procedure. You stay, I look."

"So this has happened before?" I ask incredulously. In my head I am already composing my email to the Managing Director of the company.

"Well, not to me, no," Natasha admits, starting to walk back the way we just came.

"Hang on a minute, I'll come with you," Michael says, going into hero mode. I knew he fancied Natasha.

"Absolutely not. Please stay." There's a new firmness to her voice that we haven't heard before. "This is the best way. You will all be safer here."

"Without a guide?" Diana looks anxious.

"Clive might come back here, trust me, I know what I'm doing," Natasha replies, and with a swish of her long blonde ponytail she is gone, heading back down the path and disappearing from view.

We retreat a little way into the wood to shelter from the hot sun. Diana looks like she is about to have a panic attack. Jemma looks stricken. Seamus puts his arm around her.

"This is crazy!" I say, mopping my sweating brow. "God knows when we'll see *her* again!"

"Don't say that!" gasps Jemma.

"Look, I'm sorry but you really need to keep a closer eye on your husband."

"Excuse me?"

"You didn't even know he was missing! I wouldn't call that paying attention to him, would you?"

"I told you I was talking to Seamus."

"Yes well…"

"What's that supposed to mean?"

"Charlie! Lay off her, mate, will you?" Michael puts his arm around me and guides me away from the group as Jemma starts to sob in Seamus' arms and Julie and Pam glare at me in disgust. I can feel my blood pressure rising. My doctor advised me to go on a walking holiday to help with the stress of running a multi-million pound company, not to give me a heart attack.

"This is bloody ridiculous!" I realise I'm pacing up and down. How the hell did I end up in the forty degree heat with this bunch of middle-aged no-hopers? And where on earth is that loser Clive?

"Look mate, we've just got to sit tight, okay?" Michael's a nice guy but he's as obedient as the rest of them.

"No way," I say. "We can stay here and fry or we can do something constructive."

"Like what?"

"We all need to retrace our steps until we find phone signals again. Then we can call for some proper help, get the emergency services involved."

Michael looks unsure. "But Natasha said…"

"For God's sake Michael, do you really think you're going to sell that game to anyone if you don't learn how to take charge of your own life?"

"Alright then mate, but on one condition."

"What's that?"

"You're telling them."

DIANA

I have to sit down. There is a fallen down log, a little away from the others. I sit there to compose myself. This is hell. It was bad enough when Natasha said we had another one or two hours to go, but now it's going to be who knows how long? I cannot believe she has just left us all here.

It's not just the threat of being shot, stung to death by bees or lost forever sending this feeling of panic through my body, but I cannot bear to be surrounded by these insufferable people for a second longer.

It's like I brought James with me. He and his tart are everywhere! I came away to try to take my mind away from thoughts of them and the agony of being separated from my babies. It really is like hell. My last days on earth being tormented by Mr 'God's gift to women', everybody's 'mate', and Charlie chump know-it-all. But if that's not enough we also have the mistress, in the guise of the simpering, manipulative Miss Jemma. No wonder Clive went off. Something I should have done years ago. Oh my God. I am rocking. I must stop. They will all think I have gone mad. Get a grip, Diana.

"Are you okay, Diana?" There is a hand on my shoulder.

It's Pam. "You look really stressed. Would you like some water?"

I look up and I am suddenly aware that my brow is furrowed and my shoulders tensed. She smiles gently at me, and I can't help but relax for a moment and smile back.

"Thank you. That's kind," I say. "I'm just struggling a bit."

"With the walk?"

"Yes... and a few other things."

"Let me help you up." Pam reaches her hand down and helps me to my feet. She looks across to the rest of the group and I follow her gaze. "Charlie wants us to go after Natasha."

"What? No friggin' way!" Pam looks surprised. I am a little shocked myself by the force in my voice.

I stomp over to the group and jab my finger three times into Charlie's right shoulder. As he turns round I yell at him, "Who the hell do you think you are?"

He looks shocked and, as recognition crosses his face, he stifles a laugh. Michael sniggers too.

I step back, as I too am startled when I see Charlie's face. I was half expecting it to be James. Still, I recover myself a little and continue, even though the sick feeling I so well recognise is rising inside me from my stomach into my chest and all the blood is rushing up, flushing my cheeks.

"Don't you dare laugh at me. Natasha said to wait here, so we should do as she says."

"I disagree. We can't just wait here," Charlie says.

"You presume to know better than her, do you? You..."

"What if something serious has happened, and she can't get back to us either?"

"What do you mean, serious?" says Jemma.

"All the more reason to stay," I say.

"I think I have to agree with Diana," says Julie. "What if we miss them and they come back and we're not here. It's the first rule of being found, to stay still."

"What did you mean, serious?" says Jemma. She is looking quite sick now, like she might faint. I'm even beginning to feel a little sorry for her.

"I'm sure it will be nothing," says Julie. "They'll be back soon. It's only been twenty minutes."

"Yes, you're probably right. They're probably right, Charlie mate," Michael says.

Charlie stamps his foot, like a sulky child. "Well you can all stay here then, if you like, but I am going to head back. I can't risk staying in this spot. I'm allergic to bee stings and I have forgotten my EpiPen." He strides determinedly in the direction that Natasha went. Michael, Jemma and Seamus immediately follow. I feel tears prick my eyes and my face is flushed again.

"Do you even believe that he is allergic to bee stings?" I whisper.

"Heaven knows, love," says Pam, "but we can't stay behind. I think it's best we all stick together."

I can't keep the tears back any longer. I can hardly see through them as Pam and Julie guide me in the same direction as the others.

JEMMA

Seamus keeps his hand in the small of my back, guiding me back along the path. I wish he wouldn't. I can feel the sweat running down between my shoulder blades, and I'm embarrassed by my sticky, dusty state. In fact, embarrassed is what I'm feeling generally, I realise with a jolt, as we follow Charlie's backpack bobbing ahead of us. I'm more embarrassed than worried, despite Charlie hinting that something dreadful has happened to Clive. Embarrassed, and angry. How could Clive draw attention to us like this? As if it wasn't bad enough already. Seamus keeps glancing at me. I keep my eyes firmly ahead, but he's persistent.

"Jemma, I'm sure Clive's fine," he says, panting a little. We are out of the shelter of the trees again, and the sun is piercing hot. I nod. He has to be alright. The alternatives are too awful. Seamus puts his hand on my shoulder, turning me towards him a little. He drops his voice low.

"You don't think he's, well, gone off somewhere, do you?" he glances over his shoulder, but Julie, Pam and Diana are a good twenty metres behind us.

"What do you mean?" I hiss back. I shrug his hand away, feeling my scalp prickle with humiliation.

"Look, I don't like to pry, but things seem a bit, you know, rocky between you guys. I just wondered..."

"Well don't!" I snap. I pick up my pace to get away from him.

"If you need to talk..." I hear him call after me. I don't look back.

This trip was supposed to be about wilderness, some time away from everything. Now it feels as though I'm in a goldfish bowl. I round a cluster of scrubby trees and find Charlie and Michael, rucksacks at their feet, holding their phones towards the sky.

"Still no signal," says Charlie. "Bloody foreign networks. Any joy on yours?"

"Nope," says Michael. He turns to me. "What network are you with?"

I pull out my phone, but the screen is blank. I stare at it, then remember I forgot to plug it in last night. I'd barely had the energy to get undressed after another humdinger of a row.

Charlie snorts. "Brilliant! Bloody brilliant! The one person your bloody husband is bound to try and call, and your phone is dead! Bloody brilliant!"

"Go easy, will you?" says Michael, but I can tell he thinks I'm stupid too.

I can feel the tears prickling, and I turn away to get my water bottle out of my rucksack. Seamus catches us up, crouching next to me.

"Hey! Come on, it'll be okay." He looks up at Charlie. "Have you said something to her? Can't you see she's upset?"

"Why don't you make yourself useful, Mr Lover-Boy? Have you got any signal?"

Seamus springs to his feet and lunges at Charlie. Michael grabs his arm.

"For God's sake! Can we all calm down? Seamus, your phone?" Seamus pulls it from his pocket and shakes his head. He sits down on a rock, a little way away with his back to us. Diana, Pam and Julie come puffing up the path. Pam and Julie exchange concerned glances when they see me. I pretend to search in my rucksack to avoid eye contact. Diana sinks down and takes long, deep slugs from her water bottle. She sloshes some into her palm and splashes her face.

Charlie calls over. "Don't waste your water like that! We could be out here for ages yet." Diana scowls at him.

"How much further do you think we should go?" asks Pam. "How long have we been walking? Ten, fifteen minutes? Shouldn't we have found them by now?"

Charlie seems to have appointed himself the leader of the group. "You're assuming they are still close to the trail. They could have left the route, in which case we might not see them."

"Then what the hell are we doing?" explodes Diana. "I knew we should have stayed put, like Natasha said. What's the point of having a guide if you ignore her?"

"Diana's right," says Pam. "We could be wandering around in circles for hours at this rate!"

Michael steps forward, palms out in a conciliatory gesture. "Look everyone, we weren't trying to find Clive and Natasha; we were trying to get a phone signal to call for help. Now, has anyone got a signal?" Everyone shakes their heads.

"We stay together, we press on. We find a phone signal," Charlie says. Michael nods.

We are close to the ridge now. The hot wind is whipping up dust. It's stinging my eyes and drying my mouth. I look back the way we've come, to the shady trees below us.

"I'm going back," I blurt out. "You do what you like, but I'm going back." I start off back down the trail towards the trees.

"No! Jemma! We should stay together!" calls Julie. I pretend I don't hear. I need to get away from Charlie's sneering and Pam and Julie's silent sympathetic glances. I need to get away from all of them.

Then I hear hurried steps in the dust. I glance around. It's Seamus, and behind him, on the ridge, Charlie is laughing.

CLIVE

I hear a sharp crack. What was that? I know there are hunters in these woods. Or maybe it was distant thunder. "Calm down, Clive old boy." I sometimes find that talking out loud to myself steadies me. But not this time. Instead of floating away from me, as they usually do, my words hang in the oppressive air and enlarge my feelings of isolation. This is not going to plan.

My badly twisted knee is throbbing like hell and the bee sting is causing my hand to swell up like a balloon. There is little chance that I shall be able to climb back up the steep incline towards the path at the top. I only meant to hide in the bushes by the track, but taking a tumble like this has left me shaken.

"Damn Michael." I speak out loud again. When he and I had agreed that I would 'become lost' at some point on the walk, we both grinned at the simple idea. I would be able to test Jemma's reaction to my disappearance. He would report back to me how she behaved. My unexplained absence would surely make her realise how much she depends on me. And he, in turn, would observe the group dynamics in response to a crisis, as material for the detail of his game. Brilliant. Only now I'm hurt and can't rejoin the path to follow the group. *Damn him.*

I could have told him how the others will react. Natasha will be cool and professional. She will tell the group to stay put whilst she retraces our steps. Charlie will assume leadership in her absence and do exactly the opposite from what she has instructed. Prats like him are so predictable. Diana will flip. She's a bit unstable. Seamus, the creep, will move in on Jemma. And the rest will melt into the background, unaware of their bit parts in our little drama. Except Michael, of course. He's a manipulative git. It occurs to me that I find it easy to predict the reaction of everyone except my own wife. What exactly is Jemma doing as I sit here? What else can I do to jolt her into some kind of tender feeling towards me?

"Clive? Clive? Can you hear me? Are you ok?" Natasha's distant voice interrupts my thoughts.

"Down here," I call. Within minutes, she has slid and scrambled her way down to me.

"What have you did?" she enquires, and I want to laugh. I tell her that I went behind a tree to take a pee, when I fell. As she leans over me to examine my knee, I can smell her perfume, mingled with the sweetness of perspiration. A thought occurs to me. Now that would definitely prompt Jemma into some kind of reaction. But very possibly not the one I want.

"It is good job I saw broken branches and slip marks by path. But I cannot get you back to top by my own self. I must go and get help." Natasha pulls a bottle of water out of her backpack and thrusts it into my swollen hand. I yelp in pain.

"So sorry," she says. "You have no allergy to stings, yes?"

"No," I say. "I'll be alright." After a few words of reassurance, she climbs back to the top of the incline and disappears. I lean back again, cursing my own stupidity but sighing with relief. At least I have been found before it gets dark. Overhead, I can see vultures circling. "In more ways than one." I speak out aloud again but my voice sounds strained. I hear the sharp crack again but nearer this time. It is followed by a prolonged rustling in the undergrowth not far off.

Suddenly it seems so much darker down here.

RAFA

I shield my eyes from the burning sun, as I watch a pair of vultures circling slowly. There's sudden movement in the undergrowth. The boar has decided to make a bid for freedom. I'm quick with the shotgun, but not quick enough. The boar suddenly lurches off to the left, unharmed, the gunshot ringing in my ears. The sound is followed immediately by a prolonged scream, a human scream. I break the gun and run forwards, almost certain my shot went to the left of the scream. Around the other side of a large pine sits a man.

I'm much relieved to find him fully alive, if a little out of control. He tries and fails to get to his feet.

"What the hell are you doing firing that thing?" he shouts."You could have killed me!"

"I'm shooting in my forest. What are you doing here, off the trail? Didn't you see the signs?"

He calms down a little and tells me what has happened. He's lost the rest of his group, can't walk and the pain in his knee is awful. I notice his swollen hand. No doubt one of our local bees has been busy. I need to get him to the Land Rover, but I can't manage on my own. There's another movement in the undergrowth, but it's too slow to be the boar returning.

"Clive! Clive!" It's a woman's voice. She's crying as she

emerges from the bushes, her clothing not entirely how it should be. "That gunshot! What the hell happened?"

"Jemma," is all Clive can manage to say. She sits down beside him and they embrace, awkwardly, both now crying. Slowly she seems to take in the whole scene, and turns on me. I hold up my hands and wait for her tirade to finish.

"So, do you want your boyfriend to be rescued or not?" I ask. "Perhaps you'd better check with him, before you refuse a ride home."

"What do you mean a ride home? And he's not my boyfriend, he's my hus…" She stops, mid-sentence, as another figure emerges from the undergrowth. The man looks sheepishly at the other two.

"Seamus!" Clive shouts out. "Fantastic – you've come to rescue me as well!" The walkie-talkie on my belt crackles into life.

It's Rodrigo. "Rafa! Listen, I've just spoken to Tash. Her walking group - one of them's injured. He needs a lift. Where are you?"

I interrupt him. "You're not going to believe this, but I'm with him and a couple of his walking friends right now. Rafa to the rescue eh!"

"Nice one mate. Bring 'em in. I'll get as near as I can in the Toyota and round up the rest of them. Tash says they scattered, didn't follow her instructions. She told me where to start looking."

My little group clearly hasn't understood a word of the conversation. I tell them it's their lucky day. I may be a barbarian hunter, but I'm also part of the local rescue team. Once I've strapped up Clive's knee and given him the bee treatment, we make our way very slowly downhill to the vehicle. On the way down, we come across another walker, Charlie. He stares at the struggling Clive.

"Some of this lot shouldn't be let out on a Level One walk, let alone a Level Four," he calls out. I'm not sure I fully understand what he means, but I take an instant dislike to him. I let Rodrigo know about our new arrival.

When we finally complete the rocky road journey to the hotel, they stumble out of the Land Rover, as if they've just been delivered from a warzone. Natasha's sitting by the pool, looking as cool as a lettuce, like always. But, before I have chance to say a word, they turn on her.

"What on earth are you doing here Natasha? You should be up there searching for the others, instead of chillaxing. You abandoned us! We'll have to report this."

"Why don't you ask her what she's been doing here, Charlie," I say, "instead of jumping to wild conclusions?"

"When I find poor Clive injured, I need a vehicle for him." Natasha's voice is calm and confident. "When I go back to our meeting point - nobody there. So I need a sheepdog to find you all. I decide it is best to run back here to the hotel."

"Why?" Charlie interrupts. "And how could you possibly run that far so quickly?"

"It was three miles, Charlie. One hour walk, as I told you. But I am a runner, I can do it much faster. Mobile phone useless all the time I run, but here in willage, I know there is rescue and walkie-talkie. Better than mobile. It is lucky Rafa has already found some of you. I tell Rodrigo where to search for the others and to take with him the - what do you call it in English, Rafa...?"

"Megaphone."

"Yes – megaphone. It can shout even louder than me. Rodrigo has found the others. They are on their way here now."

Charlie stalks off towards the hotel entrance. Jemma, Clive and Seamus stare at the ground, heads bowed, all aggression gone. There's a long awkward silence. I guess their holiday is over.

JERRY

Andrew Shephard

I'm hoping this isn't an obituary, but by the time you read this it might be.

Our dog, Jerry, is sick. He joined our household, or pack as we sometimes call it, in the summer of 2005. I had gone self-employed, with an office in the house, so had the opportunity to care for a puppy during the first, demanding months of the human and dog relationship. We had another Golden at the time, known as 'Old Dog', because she was. The arrival of Jerry sparked new life into Old Dog, and she happily took the puppy under her paw and taught him the ropes of domestic life. She tottered happily around with Jerry for another couple of years.

We've had a dog in the house for twenty years and the other morning, when it hit home that Jerry was very poorly, we looked at each other, my wife and I, and cried at the anticipation of loss. Watching Jerry climb on wobbly legs to the patch of grass at the top of our garden to relieve himself, summed up the bravery of animals in the face of difficulty.

As humans, we want to label the illness, to intervene, to make the dog better. We are creatures of action. The dog, this dog, wants to be left alone. Having struggled outside, he sits on the grass and conserves energy, cooled by the damp grass and the soft breezes of autumn. He tolerates the occasional stroke, a rub of the ears, a gentle brush. He shows no sign of being in pain. But he doesn't need to be with us in the way we feel we need to be near him.

Jerry was very attached to us, especially to me, because I was at home when he was a puppy; and because, to be truthful, he was a handful when he was a strong adolescent dog. He's never been shy of jumping over walls into someone's garden, or racing off when picking up the whiff of barbecued sausage or a split bag of kitchen waste three streets away. He has never grasped the concept of privacy, so any open conservatory door was an invitation to explore the house, and not everyone is a dog lover. He embarrassed me a number of times. Every time I believed he was a reformed character and let him off the lead on a familiar walk, he would play along for a few days and then go AWOL again. I don't blame him. I blame the dog's owners.

He's never taken to being put in kennels. He even hates a shut door anywhere in the house. He liked to be near us, right under my feet if possible. We did manage to keep him out of our bedroom at night, on condition that our door was open and that he could sneak in twice a year, at New Year's and bonfire night when the bangs of simulated warfare freaked him out. He would not have made a good gun dog.

One of his favourite locations was under the desk where I'm writing this piece, making it difficult for me to put my feet down. He's not there now. For the past twenty years, we've had a dog under the table when we've eaten our evening meal. Last night, Jerry was outside in the gathering gloom while we ate our chicken. Chicken, and Jerry wasn't there hoping for something to be spilled. I tell you, life feels very different at the moment.

Dogs are a messy, hairy, tying, trying, nuisance; an extra

hassle to consider for every human arrangement and engagement. They have to be walked twice every day. Sometimes they eat stuff that isn't really food and throw up on the carpet. They roll in fox poo and cow dung and horse manure, and stink the place out. They shed hair all around the house. They scratch the newly painted hallway as they roll on their back and stretch their legs, scraping paws against the wall. They bark manically at the neighbour's Jack Russell and fly into a panic if a cat enters the garden. As puppies, they destroy electronic equipment when you go out to do the shopping. As adults, they eat the newly baked apple pie left to cool (out of reach, you believed). They are a bloody, bloody, nuisance at times.

But what a wonderful relationship it is between Homo Sapiens and Canis Familiaris. I checked my Collins Gem Pocket Latin Dictionary. 'Familiaris' (adjective) means 'domestic'; and 'household', and 'family', and 'intimate', and 'friendly'. That's all dead right. As a noun, it means 'servant' and 'friend'. That's right too; though I'm not sure which one of us is the servant.

We humans give ourselves the title 'wise'. Being with Jerry through the closing chapter of his life, I'm beginning to think he's the wise one. As he gradually gives up his attachment to things domestic and focuses his dwindling strength on being a pure dog, he does not complain or struggle. He takes a lap of water from the bird bath and raises his head occasionally to sniff the evening air.

This evening I will go the Cavalry Arms and explain to the regulars why Jerry (and I) haven't been in recently. The good wishes they send him will be genuine. For all his social faux-pas, he's a very popular dog around here, greeted and patted by many. He always stopped at ninety year old Mary's front gate, whether she was out in the yard or not, because she rubbed his ears and told him he's handsome. His human friends will feel sadness. As a good vet said to us when Old Dog passed away, it's the price we pay for loving an animal who lives a shorter life than our own.

DOG GONE

Newspaper plops through locked front door
With news of great distress across the world.
No bark greets the intrusion of war and disaster.
First World problems rear their pretty heads;
Come here, go there, buy this, buy that, consume and sue.
Have something for nothing, it's your due.

But here, right here, the world is colder by degrees.
No global heat in Grimescar Valley; the people stay indoors,
Their blood unwarmed by walking marathons.

Food once gusto gobbled, rots, bagged and binned.
Black cat emboldened sits composed in a bed
Of hardy perennials, studying the bird table. Rats encroach.
Mud dries hard on boots, the body stiffens.
The museum house lies cold, quiet and clean
The roaring turbo vacuum stowed silent in the dark.

It was my companion who made the introductions
To the horses, the magpies, the jays, the acorns,
Our daily forensic examination of Blake's Promised Land.

But now no ear is cocked to listen to my poem,
No dark brown eye to monitor my mood.
I come and go unnoticed, encased in steel.

The world is changed by great events and even more by small.
"Do you miss the dog?" they ask.
Yes, naturally; and more, I miss myself.

LEIPZIG

Dave Rigby

Harz stared up at the building on the edge of the ring road, oblivious to the roar of passing traffic behind him. The street ahead looked like a normal, attractive, old-town avenue, the lime trees in full leaf, people sitting at tables drinking from coffee cups and beer glasses.

Harz felt anything but normal. He was trying to screw up the courage to go through the large wooden doors. The only other time he'd entered the building had been twenty-five years ago, under armed escort.

They'd been gathering at the church – the Nickolaikirche – for weeks, to speak out freely, a small sanctuary in a city of surveillance. He remembered clearly what they'd been told that evening. *If you're arrested, don't struggle, don't be violent, just shout out your name so we know who you are and hold your candle tightly in your two outstretched hands. They're less likely to attack you if you're holding a candle.*

And it had worked. He hadn't been assaulted. He'd been arrested and taken to the building on the ring road.

All these years later, standing on the doorstep of the building, he could still feel the terror of that cell, still smell the sweat and urine, still see the two small beds and the blocked toilet in the corner.

He took a deep breath, pushed open the wooden door and stepped into the foyer. There were tables full of leaflets explaining how the building had been used by the security service. Harz wandered in a daze through the rooms, trying to take in the displays in the glass cabinets, the recording equipment, piles of cassette tapes, a pair of slippers just like the ones he'd had to wear, a seat just like the one where he'd been photographed from three different angles, a map of the city, full of pinholes, but no pins, each hole representing a property that had been used by the long arm of the security service.

Harz tried to bring himself to look at the framed lists and photographs on the walls, to read the words describing interrogations like his own, to comprehend just how many unpaid informants there had been – thousands of them, providing information about their neighbours.

His father had warned him time and again about the risks. But his father had been from a different generation. He hadn't resented the restrictions. He'd kept his head down, worked hard at the gasworks, tilled his allotment and enjoyed a few beers at the weekends.

His father had only lived for a year after the revolution and Harz had always wished there'd been more time for them to get to know each other as adults.

Standing on the pavement once again, back out in the sunshine he found he was shaking. He needed to get to the church. He hurried through the narrow streets, crossed the Markt, passed the Altes Rathaus and only slowed his pace when he saw the spire ahead of him. He ignored the tourists inside, snapping everything in sight, and sat in a pew in the far corner, with his eyes closed, his breathing steadier.

It was his first trip back to his home town. After his mother's death, he'd immersed himself in his academic life in America and tried to bury his memories of the past. He'd become an expert on the works of Goethe, lectured at seminars and conferences, gradually developed his reputation.

But, eventually, memories of the past had wormed their way back to the surface and he'd felt unable to resist the pull of 'home' any longer.

When he finally opened his eyes and began to rise from the pew, he saw a face, one he recognised instantly - the jutting chin, sunken cheeks, something almost cartoon-like about its exaggerated features. As the figure slipped through the church door into the sunlight, Harz followed, keeping his eyes on the man's shock of white hair.

The narrow street was crowded with tourists ambling slowly in the sun, licking ice-creams, chatting and gazing in shop windows. Harz found it difficult to keep track of the white-haired man. At one point he lost him and realised he must have turned off somewhere. He backtracked, broke into a run, dodged around slow-moving pedestrians and caught sight of his man disappearing up a narrow alleyway. The cobbles were uneven and Harz had to take care with his footing. He slowed and tried to steady his breathing.

He wondered why he was chasing this man. He had no idea what he would do if he finally managed to confront him. The alley twisted and turned, the surface changing from cobbles to concrete and even to carpet for one section outside a wine shop.

The sun was dazzling when he emerged from the shade of the alley onto the main street, just in time to see the man jumping onto a tram. Harz followed, the doors slamming behind him. He slotted a euro into the ticket machine and slid into a vacant seat. The old woman next to him started talking immediately, rambling on about her husband's illness, his recent operation, how she couldn't leave him on his own, how things had been so much better in the old days. Her shopping bags fell over onto Harz's knee, but she didn't seem to notice. They travelled south out of the city, along a street where the pavements and half the road were dug up, pipes and spoil heaps everywhere. Every second building on the street seemed to be a bar or a club and Harz wondered how there could be enough customers in the city to support them all.

The tram turned left onto a suburban street, with new housing developments on either side. A roadside florist provided a brief splash of colour. When the old man started to move, Harz glanced out of the window. He recognised one of the few remaining older buildings. It was close to where his father had worked.

As the tram swept away from them, the man walked surprisingly briskly along a small tree-lined lane, past allotments and a small playground. The trees hid the gasworks until the last moment. Harz was taken aback by the sudden appearance of the circular brick structure and was once again that small boy, holding his mother's hand, waiting outside for his father to finish work. But the building looked different. There were signs and banners and a new entrance. It was no longer a gas holder but an exhibition centre. Harz followed the man into the building. He found it hard to take in how it had been transformed. He managed to work out what was missing. It was the smell that used to catch the back of his throat as a boy.

"Hey! Freidrich!" Harz didn't know how he'd suddenly

been able to recall the name. The man hesitated, turned and looked towards Harz. After staring at him for a short while, he walked off towards the café. Harz followed, took a seat at one of the tables and waited. To his surprise, Freidrich brought his tray across to the table, sat in the adjacent seat and spoke to him.

"It's Harz isn't it?" Harz was taken aback. He'd planned an interrogation in his head and now he was the one being asked a question. He nodded. "You were arrested by the Stasi, weren't you?" Freidrich spoke confidently.

"And you were the one who told them all about me!" Harz's voice was faltering. He was going on his gut feeling. Freidrich had lived a few doors away and rumour had it that he was one of the unpaid informants. Harz was sweating and he held his hands together to stop them from shaking. What was he hoping to achieve after all these years? He wasn't after some clichéd idea of 'closure'. It came as a shock when he realised he almost felt sorry for the man, the kind of man who could turn in his neighbour.

"I was the one who got you out," Freidrich said quietly. "I told them about your father, a good man, not a troublemaker. I told them how you'd been misled, how you'd fallen in with the wrong crowd. They listened to me. They knew they could rely on my information."

Harz had no idea whether the man was telling the truth. Maybe he'd dreamed up the story or maybe it had really happened like that. Freidrich held up his hand and walked away from the table, his coffee untouched. Harz watched him leave the building, the glass doors closing silently behind him.

Harz heard his father's voice telling him to go home.

FINAL CURTAIN
Virginia Hainsworth

His were dancer's feet,
not meant to walk such empty streets.
His graceful hands
now freeze around a bottle drained of good intent.

Eyes which once looked up
in theatres full of adoration,
now stare down at shoes
with holes which let all hope drain out.

That choreography of lament,
the shuffling, aching bones and leaden limbs,
shoulders hunched in grief,
from carrying no weight of love.

His pavement stage
and gutter stalls are full of litter.
His critics now the passersby who frown
and disapprove or throw a coin and not a rose.

But in his head,
applause lives on, his food of choice,
and as he fades into his cardboard home,
his dancing heart gives up the beat.

Final curtain. No encore.

SIDE DISHES

ideal reading accompaniments

SOULMATES
Suzanne Hudson

How did the writers who lunch meet? We met through an Adult Education Course at Kirklees College called 'Creative Writing for Beginners.' This is not the type of class where you 'bring a friend'. The chances are that you will be unique among your friends and they will view you with a mixture of awe and bafflement.

So we pitched up alone, a brave shot in the dark in which you trust in fate that you will find like-minded folk who will accept you and might even like you. Added to this, you will soon be reading out your work, whereby you might as well be shining a light into your soul. Risky maybe, but don't most things that are worth having in life involve an element of risk?

That introductory week we were set our first homework task, a short piece of fiction. Yes, homework. It's just like being back at school again. Old habits die hard. If you left it to the last minute then, you will inevitably do so now.

Reading out your work is at once terrifying and thrilling. You can hear your voice talking to a silent audience and you have no idea what they think, but you forge on. You will probably be shaking slightly. But something magic happens. You are making yourself vulnerable but at the same time you are connecting with others in an immediate and intimate way. Your words hit their ears and their brains instantly process them, each person interpreting what they hear in their own unique way. For those few minutes, time stops. Your classmates' varying worries and thoughts are momentarily suspended as they submit themselves to Art. There is something about it that lifts the soul of all involved.

You finish and there is a brief second where you look up from your work and half smile in embarrassment, but you also feel triumphant, like you have faced all your demons and won. You wait, adrenalin pumping around your body, for the first response. Compliments such as *I really like that* or *that's good* are jumped on and savoured like sweet treats. Relief floods your body. They like it! You didn't make a fool of yourself! You belong here, at least for this week. And now it's your turn to sit back and listen to someone else. And you know just how they feel.

THE STORY OF DARKSTONE

Dave Rigby

The title – *Darkstone* - came to me first.

What I had in mind was something mysterious, something set a few years in the future, something about a powerful security service...

I'd started writing fiction just after I retired. I had to unlearn my report-writing habits and think about plots, characters and dialogue. Two creative writing courses helped me greatly and the first short stories began to appear on my laptop.

Short stories gradually became longer stories. I wrote a couple of these before I had the *Darkstone* idea. When I started writing it in 2013, I had a rough plot in my head and a few character outlines. I never do much planning. I'm always eager, probably too eager, to start writing.

The plot developed, more characters were added and I began to feel I might actually finish the book.

I'm a regular at the Yorkshire Writers' Lunch, weekly sessions held in a Huddersfield café. We're a group of writers who are, or have been, involved in Gale Barker's creative writing courses. We talk about our writing, about reading, about trips and holidays, food and drink. When I mentioned *Darkstone*, people in the group asked me what I was going to do with it, once it was finished. I told them I hadn't really thought about it, but I didn't get away with this answer for long. Someone mentioned self-publishing, which I'd vaguely heard of, but knew little about.

So I decided to attend a self-publishing conference in March 2014. By this time I'd finished writing and editing *Darkstone.* The conference was organised by publishers Troubador, who do a lot of self-publishing work under their Matador name. That day spent in Leicester told me what I needed to know, in order to set off down the DIY publishing route.

When I reported back to the Yorkshire Writers' Lunch group, they asked me when I was going to get started. I was hesitant. Then, Emma, one of our group members, very generously offered to copy-edit and proofread the book for me.

This was just the stimulus I needed. She sent me a copy of the *Darkstone* manuscript highlighting her suggested changes. I spent a good while going through these and learning more about 'show and tell', 'foreshadowing' and 'point of view' in the process. At first it was difficult to respond to these comments. I asked myself - *what was wrong with the original?* But I quickly realised just how helpful it was to have this objective viewpoint. Once I'd incorporated the changes, I re-read the book again, hunting for any stray errors that might have escaped our combined scrutiny.

It was time to get a self-publisher lined up. I requested quotes from two firms – Troubador, as I already knew something about them and another firm, whose details I'd read about in *Writing Magazine.* Troubador provided the lower price and I made my choice.

Self-publishing is really a pick-and-mix menu. The publishers can do it all for you or you can choose to pay for some of their services and not others. You're the one who's paying and you're the one who decides. They can do the copy-editing, the proofreading, the conversion of your manuscript into a book, the printing and a whole range of marketing services – not to mention the production of an e-version!

In September 2014, I signed a contract for the preparation of my manuscript into a book format and the printing of one hundred hard copies.

I dealt, mainly, with one person at Troubador, which was really helpful from a continuity point of view. They sent me proofs of the book which they'd prepared and my job was to read these through, mark any changes required and return only the proof sheets that needed amending. This process continued until all necessary changes had been made.

I told them what I had in mind for the front cover and the first proposal they sent turned out to be just what I wanted. We agreed the author details, acknowledgements and a blurb for the back cover.

After a final check, I signed the 'send to print' form!

When fifty books arrived at my front door, at the end of January 2015, I had to contain my excitement as I slowly removed the outer packaging. Yes, they were all there and yes they looked great.

It was a relief when my first reader reported back that the book was readable and he hadn't spotted any errors!

Of course the questions from the Yorkshire Writers' Lunch group haven't stopped. Now it's all about marketing – but that's another story!

Darkstone is available from www.troubador.co.uk

ARE YOU A SCRIBBLER, A TYPER OR BOTH?

Inez Cook

I'm a bit of both.

I remember in my first weeks at university, one of my tutors laughing at those of us who still hand-wrote their work before word-processing it. "Don't worry, you'll be putting it straight onto the computer by the end of the term." She was right. It was great for academic work. It saved me lots of precious time before deadlines with its nifty shortcuts and made navigating around longer pieces of work simpler.

Ever since then, when I work straight onto a computer, I edit on the spot a lot more than when I write by hand. I have to remember to take my editing hat off otherwise I don't finish a sentence without trying out all of its other permutations. The writing and editing stages tangle themselves together. I think it's because typing straight onto the computer feels like more of a commitment. It's one step closer to having an audience and it looks like it will look in a reader's hands. I find this can be useful for writing poems. The layout of a poem is part of its uniqueness and seeing it take shape on a word document early on in the drafting process can be valuable.

With handwritten work, there's no getting away from my own scrawl. It's a slower process. The thought has to linger that tiny bit longer as I get down the last word of the sentence, something which helps to stop the editing voice popping up too soon. And there's the ache: that post-exam ache and calloused middle finger. The pain feedback that lets me know I've done a good few pages (and, if I'm lucky, a few good pages).

After writing something by hand, the editing process is much more fun and dramatic than just holding down the delete key. I can cross out a whole page with a swooping X, or scratch a word out until it's black and gone right through the paper. If more drastic measures are needed, I already have an actual piece of paper to rip, scrunch and/or throw across the room. Like at school when a paper aeroplane floats onto your desk as the teacher's back is turned: you unfold its wings to read the insult or proposition, laugh or squirm accordingly and then scrunch up the evidence. A text message tapped out from under a desk just isn't quite the same.

WAITING FOR TIME

Annabel Howarth

"Where does the time go?" It's one of my mother's catchphrases. She used to say it at the end of the long summer holidays, during my school and university days. She would sing it again, sadly, on a Sunday afternoon when we were visiting each other on a long awaited weekend, in the days when I had an office job. And, when she was at her loneliest, she would begin to sigh it out almost as soon as I had arrived, later than expected, on a Saturday afternoon. "The weekend is almost over," she would say. I would roll my eyes, impatient with her for anticipating my departure on Sunday, rather than enjoying the moment we were sharing.

But now I have children of my own - and I have chosen to be a 'stay at home mum' and, when I have the time, a writer, and I feel as though I spend so much time waiting - I get it. I have even heard those same words fall from my own lips, and cringed. I can even predict myself saying them at the end of this year's school summer holidays.

What am I waiting for? 8.50 when the school gates open and 3.15 when it's picking up time; the unknown moment in the evening when my husband will return from work; the children's bedtime, which is almost as unpredictable but mostly for the time in the in-between times, when I can do all the things which need doing, and then the things I really want to be doing, including writing.

My days seem to be eaten away, often waiting, for such

things as: my youngest child to decide he is happy to get dressed, after a half hour battle for him to stop playing with his lego or his train set so that we can go through the door; or for the children to agree that we can leave the school playing field behind and actually go home.

Following an interesting Yorkshire Writers' Lunch, I have resolved to turn over a new leaf. I shall be 'finding time' to write, rather than 'waiting for time'. That won't be confined to my usual trick of staying up until 1am and beyond, when everyone else has gone to sleep. I am not sure I can follow my colleague's 'speed ironing' routine, but other suggestions have enlightened me.

The new me has written this blog whilst sat:

a. on a garden chair in front of my house, enjoying the sunshine while the children scooter up and down, listening to their giggles, smiling and waving and keeping a cautionary eye and ear out for cars, instead of standing there and just watching and thinking about all the other things I could usefully be doing, and shouting every five minutes, "It's time to come in now!" with increasing irritation;

b. at the breakfast table, whilst the children carry out their usual painstaking routine of slowly eating their breakfast with eyes glued to the TV, without nagging them every couple of minutes to hurry up as it's time to get dressed;

c. on the toilet (closed lid!) while the children play in the bath, just a little bit longer, then run around wearing their towels like superman capes before eventually relenting to put on their pyjamas and clean their teeth, while I smile at the cuteness of it all;

d. in the pub near the village hall where my daughter is attending a party, having spent some time chatting to other parents and watching my angel have fun with her friends (who says you can't have everything?); and
e. on the sofa, next to my husband as he watches the World Cup Final, without sensing my brooding resentment (I could even bear a bit of punditry!).

It seems that 'finding time' rather than 'waiting for time' for writing, is so much more rewarding for everyone, so my idea that the school summer holidays is a time when I won't have time to write, has rather turned on its head. I am of course excited about spending time with the children and the adventures we will have, but I am also looking forward to the in-between times when I would usually be waiting. Rather than cringing when, at the end of the summer, I repeat my mother's words "Where did the time go?," I'll be smiling. It will go too fast. It always goes too fast - but this time, I predict that it won't feel wasted.

A VERY BRITISH WEEKEND
Clair Wright

A friend commented on our 'true British grit' as we set off to camp in the Peak District last weekend. Along with four other families, we defied the amber rain warning and forecast of thunder-storms, and pitched our tents on Friday evening in bright, hot sunshine. We sat enjoying our first mug of tea, watching the kids ride around on their bikes. Surely the forecast must be wrong?

Just after midnight the rain began, pattering on the canvas as we lay snug in our sleeping bags. Thunder and lightning followed, and we counted between flashes and rumbles, judging the distance of the storm. At the count of five it started to move away, and I pushed away the niggling anxiety I had been harbouring about lightning and metal tent poles.

At 6.30am we were woken by shuffling and giggling, and the boys emerged, hopping across the tent in their sleeping bags like dishevelled invertebrates. The rain was persistent, and we contemplated the dense grey cloud as we waited for the kettle to boil. Our plan to spend the day wandering around the Buxton festival in the sunshine was dissolving in the deluge.

Over breakfast we discovered that one family had abandoned their tent and gone home in the early hours, faced with the twin disasters of a nappy failure and an inconsolable toddler.

We flicked through tourist information leaflets, looking

for inspiration to keep eight adults and ten children entertained. The kids voted for the cinema, and so, feeling rather defeated, we set off for Stockport and the nearest multiplex.

A forty minute drive and lunch later, we found that the showing was full. We returned to our cars, shepherding grumpy children with promises of cinema visits in the holidays.

Back on the campsite, we sat under the shelter with another mug of tea, and I began to wonder whether 'true grit' had been the best strategy this weekend.

The kids rode around on their bikes, sprays of wet mud up their backs, hair plastered to their foreheads. I stopped trying to persuade them under cover; we had dry clothes when they needed them. They were engrossed in a complex game and the rain didn't seem to feature. No one had mentioned TV, or 'Minecraft' (their current gaming obsession) for two days.

Later, the rain stopped and the sky began to brighten over the trees. Backpackers arrived, damp but triumphant, to pitch their tents and peg wet socks to guy-lines.

With the humid evening air came the midges, and we sprayed repellent and lit citronella candles, laughing as we tucked trousers into socks.

My smart-phone had run out of charge. It had not occurred to me to charge it up; checking emails and Facebook no longer seemed that pressing. I put the kettle back on and reached for my book.

Tomorrow would be dry, and there would be no excuse for inactivity. Maybe camping in the rain isn't so bad after all.

SELF-PUBLISHING - IT'S ALL IN THE DETAIL

Emma Harding

To indent or not to indent? That is the question you never thought you'd have to ask yourself. But there are many such decisions to be made when self-publishing a book.

There are the obvious 'big' decisions - do you publish just as an ebook or produce a paperback version too or instead? How are you going to go about getting the cover designed? Who are you going to get to edit and proofread the contents?

Then there are all the 'little' decisions you never thought you'd be dithering over:

- What size is the book going to be? (Who knew there were so many options? I'm currently deliberating between 5 x 8, 5.5 x 8.5 or 6 x 9 inches).
- What font are you going to set it in? Arial, Times New Roman, Palatino Linotype, Garamond?
- What font size looks best? 10, 11 or 12pt?
- What about line spacing? Single, 1.5 or multiple 1.15?

And then there's the indenting. The convention is to indent the first line of every paragraph apart from the first one in each chapter. But my book is non-fiction and that just doesn't look right.

Because of course, that's the thing about self-publishing. It's all down to you to decide what looks right and what doesn't. If you're indecisive like me, that makes the process interminably slow and painful. You might view it as intensely boring and pernickety. After all it's the content of the book that is important, right? But I think these details matter.

Maybe, as a reader, you've never noticed what font a book's been set in. Rest assured you'd have noticed it if it had been the wrong font. If these things are done right they become invisible. They recede into the background so that the words themselves take centre-stage. Done wrong and they shout wrong so loudly you can't see the words for the text.

Imagine if you were watching a play. It's Macbeth and the cast are dressed in suitably Tudor style. Then Lady Macbeth appears and instead of wimple and gown she's wearing a purple Mohican, tutu and wellies. It would jar wouldn't it? (Although I wouldn't mind seeing that production!) Your attention would be drawn to what on earth she looks like rather than the play itself. I think it's the same with font choice, line spacing and yes, indenting.

These pernickety choices are important so that your carefully crafted words are presented to best effect. So that your reader is not distracted from the contents of your book by how it has been laid out.

So as I struggle from one decision to the next in the final stages of producing my book, I remind myself that it's all worth it for a professional-looking finished product. One where the words are front and centre.

REWRITING A SONNET

Inez Cook

This is an untitled poem I wrote in 2012. It was written in sonnet form for a creative writing class:

> My son carefully reaches for his bricks
> knocking yesterday's creation to the floor.
> Then stops mid-crawl with wide eyes and inspects
> a tiny speck of dirt beside the door.
>
> Outside he sits quite still so he can stare
> at tree-shapes and the wobbling washing line
> with pegged white sheets that billow in the air.
> Then he lifts up his arms because he can.
>
> I learn from him that stillness between action
> is what we need to grow. He's offering
> a gift; each moment is an invitation
> to see how ordinary things can sing.
>
> Remembering his eyes I see it now:
> Those sheets were ship's white sails, the lawn its bow.

At the time, I was focussing on it as a technical exercise and managed to keep to a strict rhyme scheme and metre. Rereading it recently I thought it worked as a technical exercise but the word choices were sometimes imprecise and some lines were clunky. So I rewrote it and gave it a title:

SHARED ATTENTION

My son crawls past his painted wooden bricks,
Knocks yesterday's creation to the floor,
Then stoops his head with wide eyes and inspects
A tiny speck of dirt beside the door.

Now in the garden, motionless, we stare
At tree-shapes and the bobbing washing line.
His eyes dart up at two crows' soundless flight
As pegged sheets swell and shudder in the air.

I learn from him that stillness between action
Is what we need to grow; and noticing
The world together is an invitation
To see how ordinary things can sing.

Remembering that day I see it now:
Those sheets were ship's white sails, the lawn its bow.

Rewriting it within the conventions of a sonnet felt like a really tricky jigsaw puzzle. I knew how much space I had to express each idea but some words had to be more specific and certain sentence structures needed to change. Stanza two took the most work. I took out the last line, inserted a new image about the 'soundless crows' which I had found in my original notes for the poem, and swapped the lines which slightly altered the rhyme scheme. I wanted the lines in stanza three to run more smoothly, and removed the words 'gift' and 'offering' which I felt were a bit too sentimental. I am happy with the result, but who knows, maybe in three years I'll feel the need to do a third rewrite.

FIRST WORLD PROBLEM

Andrew Shephard

I was on holiday walking through the countryside in Spain when my mobile phone broke. The screen went blank and that was it – dead. Back home, I tried a few tips from the internet, most of which involved violence towards the phone. The tips didn't work, so I went to a mobile phone shop, attracted by a special offer which was too good to ignore.

The bright and modern shop was busy. Staff in casual uniforms were attending customers browsing the latest amazing gadgets. But the happy consumer paradise was being spoiled by a man who was ranting and raving into a phone. He seemed to be trying to explain a problem to a customer service or computer expert on the other end of the connection. He spoke loudly but slowly, as if speaking to an idiot who only understood simple words. He kept repeating himself. The man's frustration was embarrassing; I saw the shop staff and customers exchange glances which said *what a rude man to speak like that.* People gave him a wide birth as if he might suddenly go crazy and lash out at them.

While I was completing my transaction, the shop computer froze and my transaction was lost in the works. The bright young assistant apologised and tried three times to get it back, blaming a new computer system that was causing some teething problems. I told her not to worry, I would return in a couple of days when it was sorted out.

Three weeks, several return visits, and over two hours on the phone to 'customer services' later, I was back in the shop. I had received an email from the Customer Service Special Team (my problem had been escalated) giving me the great news that my transaction could now be completed. I could pick up my new phone and be in touch with the world again.

The sun was shining and I walked into the shop with a spring in my trainers. The shop manager smiled at me – I had become a familiar face. But when the transaction to register my new phone would not 'go through', for a different reason this time, the clouds came over my sunny disposition. I demanded to speak to their Supreme Leader. I was given a phone to speak to Customer Services.

I began calmly enough, but after ten minutes or so of explaining, very slowly, as if I was speaking to an idiot, my voice became harsh and anger powered my words. Hearing my own account of the inconvenience, injustice, expense, lost business, lost messages, lost pictures, lost contacts I had endured, I felt a duty to put things right, to correct the glaring faults in their systems and management.

There was a pause while Customer Services attempted to transfer me to another department. I looked around the shop. Seeing the faces of the other customers and the averted eyes of the staff, I knew my fate. I had become the raving man I had seen on my first visit to the mobile phone shop.

MY PHONE IS BROKEN

I live in the age of the smarter machine
So clever, yes clever, right clever.
I'm happier talking to a human bean
But never, not ever, no never.

Glasgow, the Valleys, fair Sunderland
So concerned, so kindly, so friendly
But really it's Alice in Wonderland.
I'm helpless, quite hopeless, it's fruitless.

The bean's a small cog, a part, a device
A just-in-time manual taught to be nice,
Trained to smooth my frustration
Until I have ceased,
And accept that at least
I'm part of the beast
Not outside of the feast.
How lucky I am to be fleeced.

You live in the age of the smarter machine
It gets better and better, so clever.
Don't rave. Join us, be part of the team
Be with us, together, forever.

DESSERTS

make room for these lip-smacking puddings

LOVE ME, LOVE MY BOOKS

Clair Wright

This week has been my birthday, and my husband Richard gave me *Ex Libris – Confessions of a Common Reader* by Anne Fadiman. This collection of essays about the love of books made me reflect on my own attachment to my book collection. Why don't other objects – CDs, or clothes, for example – have the same emotional significance?

When I moved in with Richard, I brought my goods and chattels with me: half a set of cast-iron pans (the other half stayed with my ex), a dinner service (a twenty-first birthday present), and books – lots and lots of books. Over the months that followed, as we decided that this was to be a permanent arrangement, I parted with my duplicate colander (his was nicer) and my grater (ditto) and my sofa (too uncomfortable). The books, however, stayed. All of them.

My books are old friends, they are travelling companions. There are the books I have studied, laboriously; identifiable by the worn spine, the margin notes and the underlines. These are the books I could, at one time, quote at length, and whose themes, narrative technique and characterisation I have written about until I never wanted to read them again (at least, not for a while). We are like veterans of a war, these volumes and I. We have seen action, and we bear the scars.

There are those books I bought (often second hand) in a fit of academic enthusiasm, because they constituted 'reading around the text'. These are obscure collections of essays, or historical texts, books on myths and legends, or biographies. I have carted them around, they have survived six house-moves and numerous ruthless clear-outs, yet most of them remain unread. I can't part with them. To do so would be to admit defeat.

Then there are the books I just love, that I have read over and over, the stories that have stayed with me. These I might lend to a trusted fellow reader (after writing my name inside the cover), but I welcome their return like the prodigal son. To part with these would be to reject an old friend.

Richard looks perplexed. "Why do you have two copies of *Sons and Lovers*? Surely one can go?"

"Ah! No!" I exclaim, and launch into an earnest explanation of how this later edition is significantly longer than this earlier version, and is arguably truer to Lawrence's original intention. Both, therefore, are vital. Richard's eyes glaze over and he pushes them back onto the shelf.

There are similar, equally valid reasons for keeping the *Complete Works of Jane Austen* as well as most of the novels in separate volumes (the complete works is too heavy for everyday use). And for duplicates of Yeats, Joyce, Tennyson, Hardy… I could go on.

Now, with two children, the collection is growing exponentially. Books have a whole new emotional significance – how can I possibly part with the chewed board edition of *We're Going on a Bear Hunt* that we've shared together until we both know it by heart? The boys have inherited my attachment to duplicate volumes. We have two *Complete Thomas the Tank Engine* collections, containing identical stories and illustrations. We need both - the volume is part of the request – "*Gordon the Big Engine* from the red book please!" I cannot resist the draw of a box-set, so we must find room for *The Complete Roald Dahl* or several yards of *Famous Five*. Despite the lure of the internet, the boys love 'information books', weighty hardbacks called *1000 Amazing Facts* or *How Things Work* – these also must be accommodated.

When a bookcase is full, new volumes are slotted in at the top, horizontally. They pile up on bedside tables, or at the side of the sofa. I have tried to enforce a 'one in, one out' policy on myself, but to no avail. In desperation I have resorted to a Kindle, so book purchases take up only 'virtual' space.

However, Richard still buys real books for me. By his own admission, he is not a big reader of fiction. But he chooses thoughtful, luxurious reference volumes - *The Oxford Companion to English Literature,* for example, and a *Dictionary of Phrase and Fable* - both glossy tomes which take up an extravagant amount of space on the shelves. He has given me serious, thought-provoking books, indulgent, escapist books and downright silly books.

I'm off to read some more of my birthday present, as I reflect that, despite our double-stacked, groaning shelves, my husband still buys me books. That's love, that is.

THE DREAMER
Suzanne Hudson

I lie with my love while she sleeps,
Her book of poems discarded.
Even though I do not sleep, I dream.
I dream of another life for me,
Where I can paint all day.
I dream of escaping this city,
With its rows and rows of identical houses,
All crammed in, oppressive and menacing.
They suffocate me while I sleep,
So I stay awake and daydream.

In my daydreams I see myself in the country.
A cockerel crows to wake me up
And I rise immediately,
Energised by a plan that I made the night before.
Yesterday my wife picked a huge bouquet of
Wild flowers from the meadow
And arranged them beautifully in a glass vase.
Their blooms filled the house with a sweet aroma
And transformed every corner of our humble cottage
Into a place of tranquility.
I knew then that I had to paint them,
But the light was already fading,
So I resolved to do so in the morning.

I do not stop to use the washstand or change my clothes.
I do not take a drink or prepare breakfast.
I simply rise and begin.
I push the paint out of its metal tube and savour the sight
And sound of it escaping its confines.
It oozes out in a thick curly worm, onto my palette.

I inhale the smell of the oils
And a million memories dance in my mind.
Sitting at the knee of my grandfather
As he mixed his paints on this very palette.
My first tentative attempts to put paint to canvas,
With his hand next to mine,
Poised to assist.

Inspired by the painting:
Couple on a red background by Marc Chagall (1983)

FIFTY YEARS LATER

Dave Rigby

I glance at Robert as Mr Ford strides into the classroom. We don't say a word but I know he's thinking the same as me. We won't get away with anything with this one. He's just arrived at the school, the new Head of English - a solid looking man, not tall, but with an undeniable presence.

Elliot, the class joker, waits for all of fifteen minutes before putting Mr Ford to the test. I'm not sure which is his most effective weapon – the look or the barbed response, but Elliot keeps his head below the parapet for the rest of the lesson - no, the rest of the year.

For the first few weeks I find it difficult to find a way in. I wonder whether English Literature was the right choice for me. Mr Ford speaks, I listen, but nothing seems to get through. There's no connection. I write it all down, I produce the essays, he marks them and I'm unsurprised by my very average marks.

In the second term, he tells us we'll be taking the Satire Option. Now I know about satire. *That Was the Week That Was* is a weekly addiction and I'm a regular pretentious purchaser of *Private Eye*. My previously small spark of interest bursts into flame.

John Dryden and Alexander Pope are not the easiest starting point, but Mr Ford is in his analytical element. The discussion spills over into philosophy, religion, politics, and, at times, even the meaning of life. As we progress through Swift and Samuel Butler the scope for extracurricular discussion widens. We begin to develop the skills of analysis, argument, counter-argument and the carefully-crafted put-down. By the time we reach *Brave New World* and *Animal Farm* we're in full flow, not the same people we were six months earlier. Mr Ford is like a conductor, the baton moving imperceptibly.

Fifty years later I'm standing at the lectern, in the crematorium, a poem by Berthold Brecht in front of me – *Questions from a Worker Who Reads.* I look out across the sea of faces and slowly recite each line. Four of us ex-pupils, have come to pay our respects to Mr Ford, come to give our thanks for his teacher's gifts. We read from the lectern in turn and Robert tells the audience about Mr Ford's early years, his wartime experiences, his move into teaching, his love of words and language. There's no vicar, no hymns, no prayers, just people reading and talking and, to close, Liszt's *Hungarian Rhapsody*.

Afterwards over tea and cakes we go over our stories, the way we kept the links, the way John and his wife welcomed our visits, the way we all still use his teachings.

TO KISS OR NOT TO KISS

Annabel Howarth

When did saying hello or goodbye stop being simple? I'm sure it was simple when I was at school. Just 'Hello' and 'Goodbye' would suffice. The art of letter writing was quite straightforward. You only had to remember to sign off 'Yours sincerely' to a named person and 'Yours faithfully' to an unnamed 'Sir' or 'Madam'. When I recently received a text from a burly builder friend, apologising for not having put a 'x' at the end of his previous text, it made me laugh out loud, but also had me thinking how complicated it has all become, and what an awful waste of emotional energy we must expend trying to get it right.

I think I was first aware of the issue in the sixth form when some of the drama luvvies started to air kiss when they met each other. Being air kissed for the first time was quite a shock and straight out of my comfort zone. I struggled with that through university and into the work place. Is it the right thing to actually kiss on the cheek or do we just make that smacking sound and brush cheeks? Is it one cheek or two? And the amount of times I've had an awkward moment when accidentally brushing lips with someone is too embarrassing to think about for more than a second. Thankfully there is no air kissing at the school gates that I have noticed, so that is one problem I seldom face these days.

The art of letter writing seemed to become a problem when communication moved into the realm of emails. Less formality meant I was suddenly faced with a new dilemma in the workplace. Did I greet my boss with a 'Dear' or a 'Hi'? I think one eventually morphed into the other, and also with clients. How and when did that happen? It seemed natural to end each email with a short and sweet 'Thanks'. Over time I cottoned on to 'Regards' which at some stage was met with 'Kind Regards', 'Warm Regards' and 'Best Regards'. When does one become the other? Now I flinch when someone sends me a message with simply 'Regards'. What does that mean? It somehow feels so cold, especially if it is in response to my 'Kind Regards' but then what does the sender intend? Perhaps they always sign off 'Regards' and it means nothing at all. I also became unsure of the adequacy of my 'Thanks' when I started to receive the dreaded 'Many Thanks'.

At one point I remember receiving a 'Best' and was sent off-kilter. Best what? Since then all 'regards' seem very business-like and having come out of the business arena, I find myself never quite sure how to sign off an email, often signing with 'Best wishes' but can't help but feel those words sound like something off an outmoded Christmas card. So for me the dilemma continues.

I will never forget the backstabbing 'S'. He was a lawyer acting on the other side of a deal. My stomach flipped when I received a message in such an over-familiar way. Was his name Simon or Stuart? I forget, but his overfamiliarity was just a trick to make me believe we were on the same team. "Thanks S," I thought when he tried to make me look a fool in front of my client later down the line. No more 'A' sign offs for you from now on.

The biggest struggle for me, however, is the 'x' problem.

Almost everyone seems to sign off their text messages with a 'x' and that same shoulder-tightening flinch creeps up on me when I receive a message without a 'x', or if I forget to send one. They seem so overused now that the receipt of a 'x' has lost its currency. It's more of an issue not to receive one, than a joy to receive one. Some of my old work colleagues don't 'x', or only very occasionally. Receipt of a 'x' from them seems to hold more meaning. At least backstabbing 'S' didn't resort to signing off with a 'x'!

Not satisfied with one 'x', there is now the double 'x' or the triple 'x'. Recently I found out that some people have 'xxx' set up as an automatic response. The overuse of the 'x' is becoming as unnecessary and meaningless as the overused '!'. Maybe we should go back to a more sincere 'Hello' and 'Goodbye' - no air kisses please - an emailed 'Hi' and 'Thanks,' and I guess I will just have to put a 'x' on my text messages each and every time, just to be on the safe side, along with my burly builder friend.

CHALK

Clair Wright

Pleats swinging, square heels pick across the school hall
She lifts the needle, the music stops.
Ageless, yet ever-middle-aged
Face pink, scrubbed, brisk,
Hair neat from its weekly set
She surveys us in our cross-legged rows.
The conductor of an orchestra, she opens
With an overture of "good mornings"
Chorused in unison.
She directs, with an eyebrow,
The teacher at the piano stool
A cheery hymn to sunshine and obedience.
One hundred faces raised to hers -
Deliverer of stern words, gold stars, boiled sweets,
The epitome of school.

But then
For two summer weeks, a revelation:
Marooned in the hall, a single table, set for one,
With ceremony, the television set
Resplendent on its trolley
Is wheeled in place.

Unmindful of two hundred wondering eyes,
Of clatter and chatter, spills and splatter,
Dining alone on shepherd's pie and treacle sponge
But tasting strawberries and champagne
She is absorbed
In the drama on the grassy stage
Of white-clad gladiators of racket and ball
And we glimpse the unimagined
Life beyond.

AN AFRICAN NIGHT

Virginia Hainsworth

Just for a moment, take some time out from writing, or thinking about writing, or reading about writing, or avoiding writing and let me take you somewhere else. For a few seconds, let me whisk you away to the depths of... *An African Night*

The dense black sky holds you tightly in its grip. It tempts you with effervescent stars, beckoning you to faraway galaxies.

As you gaze up at worlds which are long dead, the sounds resonating here below remind you of life on the edge. The distant throaty, rumbling roar of a male lion proclaiming his territory. The whoop whoop of snorting zebra, uneasy at the presence of predators. The honking sound of hippos emerging from their jacuzzi to take a midnight stroll and check out their favourite eating places. The small pond, quiet and peaceful during the day, now allowing its population of frogs to raise their voices in a chorus of amphibian passion, their love songs filling the air.

The hubbub of sounds that lets you know that this is no ordinary night. This is an African night. It is bursting at the seams with life. You cannot see any of it under the inkiness of the moonless sky, but you can hear it everywhere. You are reminded how microscopic you are in this wonderful place, this birthplace of humanity, this land boiling with delights. This Africa.

SONGS IN THE KEY OF ELLA
(aged three months)
Inez Cook

I love it when my big brother, Eric, sings to me. He must love it too, because he does it lots. Sometimes I join in and sing with him. Then he says, "don't interstruddle me!", which I think means he prefers me to listen. Here's the song he did the other day:

> Georgie Porgy went to Gloucester
> In a shower of rain.
> He stepped in a puddle
> Right up to his middle
> And frightened Miss Muffet away.

I don't know about you, but I reckon he's been sellotaping those words together like he does with his bits of paper.

***

Mum sings to me too. She likes to do it while she's rocking me:

> Lu-la, lu lu-la,
> Lu-la, lullaby.
> Lu-la, lu lu-la
> Lu-la, …

(no matter how hard I try, I can never catch the ending.)

Dad's songs are a bit more upbeat. His favourite goes something like this:

> Hello Ella Ella
> Hello Ella Manuela Ella (repeat)

Neither of us knows who Manuela is, but hey, it rhymes. This one goes faster and faster until one of us smiles. If Liverpool has just won, he makes me smile. If Liverpool has just lost, I make him smile.

***

Here's a little song I wrote about my brother's baking skills. You'll probably know the tune. It works quite well if you march along to it too:

~~THE GRAND OLD DUKE OF YORK~~
MY BROTHER MADE A CAKE

> My brother made a cake
> With playdough he had found.
> He squished it into a pancake shape
> Then he lay it on the ground.
> And when he was done he declared,
> "A cake for your wedding, come see!"
> And there, as my 'groom', on the top of the cake,
> Stood an Obi-Wan figurine.

IT'S THAT TIME OF YEAR

Virginia Hainsworth

The tick-tocking of the clock reminds me how long each dragging second takes to release its hold on time and hand over to the next. The red second hand slips down the clock face. It is not allowed to pause at the bottom before it must begin its uphill trek once more. If I watch it, one minute is an eternity. I take my gaze away and concentrate on the task in hand. When I look back at the clock a few minutes later, or so it seems, I feel sure that it has cheated me and skipped forward twenty-fold, extinguishing many precious minutes of my time.

I look down once more at the question paper and the words jump about on the page. I stare at them and they settle down, allowing me to see into them. I reach into my mind. Nothing there. And then suddenly, butterfly thoughts are released and they fly around in all directions, bumping into each other within the confines of my brain. I wait for a moment until, one by one, they come to rest in ones and twos and threes. Carefully, I pick them up and try to put them into words.

Sometimes, the words tumble out onto the paper and arrange themselves. Sometimes, they need a little help. It is then that I look out of the window. The distant horizon beckons me. *Leave now and join me,* it calls silently. I am tempted. The hills are pale in the morning sunshine, rested from their sleep. But they will soon awaken and dress themselves in purple and emerald. I want to fly to them.

But no. I force my gaze downwards to the half empty page and resolve to fill it before I allow myself to look up again.

For the most part, the other sounds in the room distance themselves from me, remaining on the borders of my consciousness. But occasionally they slip into my awareness. The rustling of paper. The creaking of chairs. Sniffing. Scribbling. I try not to look around, for if I see people writing furiously, I am alarmed by their rate of output. Someone asks for extra paper. Oh my goodness, I must write more. Someone else puts their pen down and folds their arms. They have finished. Gosh. I must speed up.

And so, eventually I am done. One final trawl of my scoured brain to see if anything else is lurking there - maybe a final phrase or piece of wisdom which I need to tip out onto the paper. And then, just in time, I ceremoniously put my pen down and listen for the long awaited words.

"That's it. Your time is up. Please stop writing and put your pens down."

A HAPPY MARRIAGE?

Suzanne Hudson

I love a mystery. There's something about one that captures my imagination and like a dog with a bone, I can't let it go until I've solved it. You never know when you might stumble across one. On a recent visit to Harewood House, near Leeds, a chance remark by my mum ignited something, which then took hold of me for the next three days.

Harewood was the home of our present Queen's Aunt, Princess Mary, only daughter of King George V and Queen Mary. She married a wealthy aristocrat, Henry Lascelles, the 6th Earl of Harewood, in 1922.

We were just nearing the end of our tour of the house when Mum told to me she had previously read that Princess Mary was unhappily married and that her much older husband could be 'cold and abusive'. She said that there had been rumours that Mary did not want to marry Lord Lascelles, that she had been forced into the marriage by her parents and that Lascelles had proposed to her after a wager at his club.

Her brother the Prince of Wales, later King Edward VIII, to whom she was very close, was said to be against the marriage because he did not want his sister to marry someone whom she did not love. She had apparently 'cried her eyes out' the night before the wedding.

Princess Mary was no longer this distant figure from history, she had become real to me, human and tortured. I wanted to know everything about her, right now.

Thank God for the internet. Back home that evening, it took just a few clicks and my search began. Within seconds up popped specialist websites, by people with a fascination with European royalty. I obsessively trawled through blogs and forums, scanning the text for any titbits of information that would confirm or deny the rumours about Mary. Hours passed. Just when I was about to tear myself away and go to bed, I hit upon a nugget of gold. Someone called Angele had posted the following comment on a thread about Mary's marriage:

"It is my understanding that Mary was very much in love with Walter Montague Douglas Scott, son and heir to the Duke of Buccleuch and these feelings were reciprocated. Unfortunately though, for various reasons, it was not thought to be a suitable match. I do think that Mary made the best of the situation, probably helped by her sense of duty, which I believe she had in abundance."

The romantic in me wanted to believe that Mary had known true love before she had to marry Lascelles. My imagination was now running riot, visualising Mary homesick and miserable at Harewood, pining for her lost love. Further research revealed that Mary's brother Henry ended up marrying Walter's sister Alice. Mary and Walter must have met again in later life. Was the spark still there? Did their eyes ever meet across a crowded room? And did Mary, who had always been taught to negate her own feelings, ever wonder, what if?

SIX TREES

Andrew Shephard

Walking through a woodland maze, I see you
A sapling bending freely with the breeze.
Slender limbs reach for blue skies,
Your roots seek hidden seas.

Beside a chattering stream, I see you
A willow dressed in flowing green.
Moved to song by sparkling water,
You harmonise its diamond dreams.

In summer's hazy meadow, I see you
A chestnut, branches draped in home grown cloth.
Children, grass, and flowers, play around you
Comforted by a show of permanence.

On a rock-strewn hillside, I see you
Battling rowan, strong against the storm.
Standing separate, but not alone
Red berries decorate your crown.

Guarded by tall pines, I see you
Red sycamore clothed in autumn leaves.
Your seeds, a twirling party of flight,
Send kindly signals across the land.

Darker now, but still I see you
A birch frozen silver by the moon.
Wearing bright rings of wisdom lightly,
Straight towards the stars you grow.

Some no longer feel the warmth of sunshine.
Some are chopped down, untimely, for the fire.
May green leaves return for you each spring
To bathe you once again in solar power.

DIGESTIF

loosen those reading buttons
with this aid to digestion

LAGO D'ORTA, PIEMONTE

Emma Harding

A golden afternoon, light shimmering on the water.
Our post-prandial stroll arrested by the view -
A line of pontoons staple the lake to the shore,
Ancient forested mountains loom vertiginously,
And patches of terracotta dwellings
Huddle round tall bell towers.

You swim, I watch.
Easing your way from the warm shallows to deeper water,
Your pale skin stark against the inky green depths.
With a flick of your legs you dive underneath,
Bubbles wobble to the surface and break.
Later, stretched out to dry, droplets from your hair spot the sun-bleached wood.

That day, on the shore of the Lago d'Orta,
We were held by the warmth of the sun,
Soothed by the rhythmic slap of gentle waves,
Mesmerised by the movement of light on water.
It was still and calm,
We were restored.

PETIT FOURS

indulge a sweet tooth with these dainty treats

THE SIGH OF THE BEHOLDER

Andrew Shephard

I can't wear that hat, it makes my face fat
Baring the shoulder makes me look older
Why do you want me to dress up bolder?
Mutton dressed lamb is not where I'm at.

Try it on, lover; don't think of the price,
Add scarf or coat if weather is colder
You look quite the part (that's what I told her)
I swear on my life, it makes you look nice.

But fabric's flimsy, my waist is thicker…
Then take all off, right down to the knicker
I'll admire your fine body without a snigger
All wrinkles smoothed by candle's flicker.
Close your eyes gently 'fore you grow older
And feel my soft sigh on your bare shoulder.

DAISY – A POEM RECREATION

Inez Cook

This poem is part of a task I did for a creative writing class. We had to take an existing poem and 'recreate' it by thinking about the essence of the original but then making something new. The original poem I chose is 'Daisy' by Alice Oswald, from her collection *Weeds and Wild Flowers* (2009).

DAISY

I'm chosen, picked,
My dirty feet no longer
Snugly in mud.
Higher than ever,
I feel the cold air
Batter my lashes.
You set me down on
The palm of your hand,
Warm as a nudging worm,
And push your thumbnail in.
Our limbs are looped.
You lift us up to have a look.
Now I hang in mid-air, held,
To serve your summer
With my eye shut tight.

ITALIAN IMPRESSIONS
Emma Harding

First thing: the drone of a motorcycle, the rattle of shutters being raised, someone pushing a trolley along the street, full to the brim with bottles of water. A man calls out a greeting to his neighbour, who crosses the street towards him. They stand together, strenuously discussing the news, the weather, food, family - who knows? It's not a language I understand beyond the stock phrases - hello, goodbye, please, thank you, the bill etc. The street is shiny - did it rain last night or has it been cleaned? The sky is bright blue, the sort of blue that proves you're on holiday, the sort of blue that promises a dry, warm day.

Street-watching: a plethora of smells - cigarette smoke, diesel, drains, plus coffee, jasmine, ozone, garlic, oregano. Bread oven at full pelt, the queue pushing out the door and into the street. A stray dog lollops past, he's carrying a plastic bag as if it contains all his worldly possessions. He disappears down a side street. There's a guy sat on the church steps playing an accordion, a bowl by his foot. A gaggle of schoolchildren, all wearing red caps bearing their names, gather at the entrance. Some take pictures, a trio of girls sit down, while a couple of lads lark about, playing tag. A teacher gathers them together and they make their way, haphazardly, groups forming, pulling apart, then reforming, along the street, to the gelateria. Then there is a scramble of caps, arms, as ice-creams are selected, produced and devoured. The dog returns, following the same route as before, still carrying his bag.

Siesta: the cool dark bedroom is like respite. The bed neatly made, fresh towels in the bathroom and fresh water in the fridge. The simplicity of the room - just functional furniture, no ornaments or pictures, no patterned furnishings, the shutters keeping out the heat - is somehow calming, cleansing. Like the day has been washed away.

AFTERNOON TEA

time to put your feet up with a nice cup of tea
and a piece of cake

DARJEELING DARLING

Andrew Shephard

"Cup of tea?"

Please, and make it with loving laughter.
The ease of dusty sweepings I don't deny,
A bag tossed carelessly into tepid water
And stirred to thickness with sweetened milk.
But are we not New Age tea drinkers, you and I?

"We are. For you, I will make posh tea.
I will fly to Darjeeling,
Swoop down from an icy ridge,
To alight on a distant continent
Like a crested migrant on a burnished bush.
I will buy a golden packet, neatly folded, tied with string,
From the youngest estate, rare and tender,
And brew for you the choicest summer flush."

You go.
I fill the kettle, remembering your exquisite flavour.
Yours is a light perfume, your leaves palm-rolled,
Best relished pure.
Beauty is soaked deep into your fabric,
Like tannin on a teacloth.
Will I taste your golden tips, unclouded?

Will I quench my thirst from your tender cups?
Will I drink again your heady muscatel brew,
Scalding my tongue on your boiling heat?

Here's why you must return with tea in your luggage:
In truth it's not the first flush, nor the second,
Not even the languid longing of oolong;
But when we age together,
The heart remains young.
Avoiding milk and sugar we will live forever
Cured of all fears,
Guarded by the ceremony of pot and leaves.

WRITING AS A GIFT

Virginia Hainsworth

To write is to present a gift to the reader. And, like any other gift, it can take many forms.

There is the gift designed 'just in case'. It is not particularly special. It is for just about anyone who comes along unexpectedly, any number of potential recipients, suitable for a wide variety of readers. It sits in your 'gift drawer', or your computer, waiting for the right opportunity to be given. It may be edited slightly – or re-wrapped – before being presented, so as to appear customised.

Then there may be the gift which you quite like yourself but are not sure if the intended recipients will. So you hang on to it for a while until you can decide whether or not it will ever see the light of day. But, because you are a writer, you really must pass it on, otherwise what is the point?

There is, of course, the gift which you wrote ages ago and with which you are not particularly pleased. It lies around for a long time, unwrapped, unfinished. You may tinker with it from time to time, sometimes making it worse or sometimes, eventually, making it presentable. So you offer it, but tentatively. And not to loved ones. And you make sure that you are not around when it is opened.

You may give a gift to yourself. It contains part of you, part of your innermost thoughts, intentions desires or regrets. It is never intended to be opened by anyone but you. It is your journal and must be kept safe, hidden from prying eyes.

I trust you are not the sort of writer who takes a gift which you received from someone else and rewraps or edits it slightly, before giving it as a present to others. It is called plagiarism, you know and will land you in hot water!

Because you are a writer, however, the gift you most love to offer is the one which everyone is clamouring to receive. You have planned it well, designed it carefully, wrapped it beautifully. It is appealing to look at, to dive into, to savour and devour. It is enjoyed by many, by all manner of recipients and stays with them for a long time. And you might even have been paid to give it!

Finally, there is the best gift of all. The one which you have developed with passion. You have crafted and honed it carefully. It is given with love. It is a unique gift because it has only one, very special, recipient. It is a love letter, or a poem for someone's special birthday or special event. It is not to be shared with anyone else.

So go on… give a very special and personal gift. To one person or a million and one. Just write.

MEET THE CHEFS

Andrew Shephard

Baker's delivery man, joiner, probation officer, manager... and writer; these are just some of the occupations providing material for the articles, stories, poems and novels which appear at the end of Andrew's fingers. Having combined writing with paid work, he now combines it with a garden and a dog. Andrew's publications include a guide for social workers and a fantasy series published under a pen-name. His latest novel, *Nellie and Tabs*, about two young hippies finding their way through the 1970s, will be published in 2016.

Annabel Howarth

Annabel has enjoyed creative writing ever since she learned how to write. As a child she was taken with the character of Jo in *Little Women* and imagined her life as a novelist. In a moment of teenage madness and having watched too much *LA Law*, she turned her attention to the pursuit of a legal career, studying and eventually practising company commercial law. When her daughter was born in 2008, her creative ambitions were reignited and her career focus is now on fulfilling her earlier dreams as a writer. Annabel enjoys writing children's stories, short stories, poems and articles.

Clair Wright

Clair has finally got around to writing something of her own, after spending a lot of time writing about other people's writing, as a literature student. She enjoys writing poetry, short stories, and articles and attends a weekly creative writing class for motivation and inspiration. She also co-writes and edits a monthly e-magazine, *Saxophone Life*. She is also a mum, a school governor, works part-time and has a very understanding husband!

Dave Rigby

Dave started writing shortly after he retired six years ago. With the benefit of two creative writing classes, he began with short stories and gradually one or two of these got longer. He self-published his first book, *Darkstone*, in 2015 and is finalising a second one, *Shoreline*, for later this year. Dave really enjoys writing for the Yorkshire Writers' Lunch blog, especially having the discipline of a 600-800 word limit and yet the freedom to write about anything. Our collaborative writing experiments are, for Dave, a very welcome development.

Emma Harding

Mild-mannered freelance copywriter and editor by day, voracious reader by night, Emma has always been struck by the power of words - to sell, persuade, enthuse and ultimately to tell stories. It has taken a long time though to find the right place to take her first faltering steps as a nascent fiction writer. The Yorkshire Writers' Lunch is that place. Not only has the support she found there led to stories, poems and Italian-inspired musings but also to the confidence to self-publish *Thinking about fostering? A practical guide*, a book based on 15 years spent helping organisations recruit foster carers.

Inez Cook

Inez grew up in Oldham, Greater Manchester. Her love of language began while listening to her parents' home-spun tales and later at school thanks to an English teacher who opened doors to the world. After graduating she worked in bookselling, libraries and then adult education. She has lived in France and Kosovo and now lives in Huddersfield. She writes poetry, short fiction and non-fiction. Since having children she has become a picturebook enthusiast and can often be found cross-legged on the floor of her local library, son in lap, captivated by storytime.

Suzanne Hudson

Suzanne lives in Mirfield, West Yorkshire with her husband and two children and works part-time as a supply teacher. Her love of writing developed from her love of reading and she began writing at a young age. When she was eight years old she wrote a play based on the children's story *The Very Important Man* and persuaded her sister and friends to perform it with her in the back garden. Suzanne has a degree in English and Communication Arts. In 2012 she plucked up the courage to begin a creative writing course at Kirklees College. She enjoys writing short stories and articles and has been published in the *Times Educational Supplement*.

Virginia Hainsworth

Virginia is an aspiring writer who loves to travel. No surprise, then that she particularly enjoys travel writing. Her aim is to enable readers to journey far and wide, all from the comfort of their own armchairs. She also loves to write poetry, drawing inspiration from many sources, more recently the centenary of the First World War. Her short stories are often inspired by her travels and some contain a poem or two. She has no intention of writing a novel, but then she has done lots of things in her life which she never intended, so who knows?

ACKNOWLEDGEMENTS

Whilst we have no one but ourselves to blame for the contents of this collection, we would like to thank Tori and the cheerful crew at the Blue Rooms, Byram Arcade, Huddersfield, for great food and a table every Tuesday; Gale Barker, creative writing tutor at Kirklees College, who gave us the nerve to get started; the friends, partners and readers who have encouraged, or at least tolerated, our writing habit; and the patient people who have chopped, sorted, arranged and picked over the words so that they appear in roughly the right order, especially Mandy, Annabel, and Emma.

YWL

37519807R00118

Printed in Great Britain
by Amazon